LIFE BEFORE DAMAGED VOL. 1
THE FERRO FAMILY

BY:

H.M. WARD

www.SexyAwesomeBooks.com

COPYRIGHT

LIFE BEFORE DAMAGED VOL. 1

PROLOGUE

PETER

THE PRESENT

Sidney nervously twists her engagement ring on her finger and looks up at me. In that soft voice, the one she uses when she's worried, she asks, "What'd you find?"

The pit of my stomach has been in freefall all day, ever since I opened that last box. It was hers—Gina's. After everything we went through, I never realized Gina kept a journal, an account of everything, including vivid descriptions of the man I once was. Sidney knows about my reputation, but what was printed in the tabloids and what's written in these diaries are two very different stories.

It's strange being in love again. I thought I'd die alone. After I lost Gina, I had no aspirations, no hope. Then Sidney changed my life. Holding these books makes me feel my old self, still there, buried deep within. All the rage, the fights, the never-ending line of women who would do anything to fuck me—in these pages, the memories are vivid. As each remembered moment blurs by, I feel the impact, the void of the person I was screaming out from deep within. But that period of my life is over, lost to the past, and I force the echoes of who I was to be quiet once more.

Truth be told, I don't miss that life, but I worry about what will happen when Sidney discovers who I was, what I was. Sidney thinks the best of me. She sees me as the English professor, the poet. But deep within, I'm not him. This part of my past lurks within me still. It reared its ugly head when Sidney's ex tried to hurt her. I made him pay for that. My violence was justified, but it doesn't matter. At the end of the day —even though I changed my name—I'm still Pete Ferro.

Glancing at the journals in my hands, I make the choice. She needs to know. If Sidney is marrying me, she needs to see the good and the bad. Reading it from a tabloid isn't enough. Swallowing hard, I cross the room clutching the books tightly.

I look around the little house Sean gave us, thinking, yet again, how perfect it is— right down to the custom made perch for Mr. Turkey. Sometimes Sean acts so stoic I think he doesn't give a shit about anyone or anything, but then he does something like this. I can't figure him out. When I see Sean and think of his life, I wonder how similar we really are; I wonder if the only reason that I'm different is because I pretend to be.

Is that all it takes to change? Maybe I'm not different after all, maybe I just want to be. A different last name, a different life— one that isn't etched with scars and faded dreams. When I look at Sidney I feel alive again. The ghost of who I was disappears and I'm real—every wish, every dream able to come true, all because of her. Showing these journals to her could destroy us, but hearing the truth about me from someone else would be so much worse. I won't take that chance.

Sidney is sitting on the bed, solemnly waiting for me to speak, as if she can sense the weight on my soul. I'd thought my soul was irretrievably lost until Sidney sat down at my table and flashed that beautiful smile. Thank God for her.

"Sidney?" Although I try, I can't hide my feelings from her, I never could.

"Peter, what is it?"

I sit down facing her, making the bed dip beneath my weight, and place the books on the comforter between us. "While I was going through my old things, I found these —they're Gina's journals." My voice catches and I look everywhere except at Sidney. Sucking in air, I push through. I need to say this before the hole in my chest consumes me. It's growing, adding pressure that wasn't there a moment ago. It scolds me, urging silence.

She won't understand, a voice says in the back of my mind. It latches onto times that I tried to tell the truth and it bit me on the ass. Ice forms, freezing my skin from the inside out, until I shiver.

Sidney places her palm on my hand. It's warm and steady, firm and fragile. She looks up at me with those dark eyes and I want to melt into her. I want to shove these in the trash and run, but I can't. No matter how hard I try, I can't change who I was—who I am.

She has to know.

I manage a half-smile as I look down at her. "While I was unpacking, I found a few old boxes that I never opened after the last move. They were relics from an old life, a past that I didn't want to remember." I pause, trying to muster the strength to say the rest and hand over the books. My jaw tightens as if my body knows this is the fastest way to kill our relationship, but my heart protests. It speaks, forcing the words over my lips, "When I opened it today, I found these books. They're Gina's journals."

Sidney's mouth drops, forming a little O, as a whirlwind of emotions play across her face. Her grip on my hand tightens as she leans in. "Oh, my God. Peter, I'm so sorry. That must have been hard." She reaches forward, taking my other hand, trying to comfort me, but that's the last thing I want right now.

Tipping her head to mine, our foreheads touch. I quiet myself, holding her hands, breathing her in, allowing myself to get intoxicated with her scent—her touch. A smile plays on her lips and one of her hands reaches around my neck. She rests her wrist on my shoulder while her fingers play with the hair at the nape of my neck. It's a Sidney motion of kindness, making me want to pull her to my chest and never let her go.

Ever since she found out that I was actually a Ferro, she's been nothing but kind. With the upcoming wedding, Sidney didn't even ask me to drop Gina's last name. She would take Gina's last name too if I asked her to, I know she would. Sidney understands loss in a way that many can't. That's why withholding this part of my life from her isn't right. I don't deserve her.

This is my only chance. It could backfire horribly, and yet, it feels right. Pulling back, I shove my hands through my hair and let out a rush of air. "The thing is, these diaries are about me, about who I was before we met. The guy in the papers doesn't hold a torch to the asshole I used to be, and Sidney, he's still here." Leaning in toward the books, I tap one of the covers. "This guy is still part of me."

From the look on her face, I know she doesn't believe me. It's not that she thinks I'm lying, but it's compassion and forgiveness given unknowingly. I take her hand and absently toy with the stone on her ring. "This is something that you need to know. I'm not the man I was before, but he's still here, buried inside. Asking you to read these is strange, I know. It has the thoughts of another woman and—"

Sidney reaches out, stands, and places a finger on my lips. My heart aches so badly it feels like it may explode. "Shhh. Peter, you aren't the guy you were before. Anyone can see that. Hell, even Sean can see that and he's an asshole." She drops her hand and offers a small smile. "Everyone has a past, even me. We don't have to do this."

"Your past is different. You didn't willingly, knowingly do bad things. I did. If you're going to marry me, if you want to truly be with me and understand my shadows, my faults, and help me from slipping back into the man I was, you need to read these."

My stomach twists into knots saying this to her. There's a million different ways she could take this new information, and I have no idea how much detail Gina went into about how I treated her, what she saw, and what I did. I couldn't bring myself to read more than a few pages. Each one was about how messed up I was and how much she hated me. I was cruel to her, and there was no reason, no excuse. Gina painted me as the perfect storm, glorious to behold and equally deadly, destroying everything in its path without remorse or shame.

Sidney takes the first book and nods. "I'd do anything for you Peter, but no matter what's in here, it won't change my mind about you, about us."

"I wouldn't be too sure about that." Stepping back quickly, I shove my hands in my pockets and dart out of the room before she can respond.

THE WAREHOUSE RAVE

GINA

JUNE 28TH, 7:33 pm

"I can't believe you talked me into this Erin!"

I'm screaming in my bestie's ear, standing in the middle of an old warehouse. A throng of wealthy twenty-somethings are laughing and dancing all around me. Well, suggestively grinding and rubbing up against each other to the unrelenting and deafening beat of the music is more accurate. It feels like a furnace in here, and the open windows don't help. Beads of sweat drip between my shoulder blades, soaking the back of my perfectly pressed white sleeveless blouse. If I had decent breasts—which I don't—I'd probably have a river rushing through that valley.

Looking around, I let out a discouraged sigh. At least people are still somewhat dressed, with the exception of a few scattered groups of hardcore ravers. Spying them makes my jaw drop. The girls are dressed in two-piece latex swimsuits, of various neon colors, showing off way too much skin. But what makes my eyes bug out of my head isn't their lack of clothing; it's the huge, knee-high, furry leg warmers. I'm talking Abominable Snowman, fluff fest. Eskimo boots have nothing on these leg warmers. One girl even has a huge fluffy cat hood to match her furry paws, uh, I mean legs.

As for the men, lots of them are decked out in glowing baggy pants, with blinking lights, and glow-in-the-dark neon tattoos on their backs and chests.

Catwoman's date has cat feet that poke out from under his baggy pants and he's wearing a headband with cat ears... that twitch. WTF? I totally missed the dress like a lunatic memo.

In the hopes of pulling off the wallflower thing, I opted for blandness—jeans and a white blouse. But instead of blending in, I stand out like a nun in a whorehouse. My blouse glows under the black lights and since I'm wearing much more fabric than anyone else here, I look like a freaking glow stick.

Wait, it gets better. Some of these people are way over the indecent exposure line, and I'm increasingly worried that the sex police, or just the regular police, will bust down the doors and haul our asses to jail. My ass is too pretty for jail. Nerves flitter through my stomach as I clutch my cell phone tightly, hoping that it won't crack into a million pieces. If I had a nametag, mine would say: Hello! My name is: Neurotic Mess.

Truth is, I can't get caught and I'm not badass enough to say fuck it and do whatever I want, like those chicks with the glowing boobs. Seriously? What the hell? Clothing isn't optional, and I should know, because this is my godforsaken rave.

Erin, my BFF, is standing beside me, dressed in paint-stained denim overalls. A pink neon sports bra peeks out from under the denim and she's got glow-in-the-dark bracelets from wrist to shoulder. She's even more of a sweaty mess than I am, but on her it looks great. Her dark, damp hair curls a little and hangs in chunks around her face. My hair has gone to frizz ball hell—so much for my perfectly curled hair from earlier this evening.

Erin bumps her shoulder against mine and gives me an exaggerated sweet smile. "Don't worry, Regina. Everything will be fine. Take a chill pill and dance!"

My head whips around fast enough to give myself whiplash. Erin ignores me, smiling and dancing by herself, moving her hips suggestively as she touches herself inappropriately. It looks like she's copulating with a ghost. It's obscene, but she pulls it off. All she needs is a pole, and the effect would be complete.

I move closer to her and yell, "A chill pill? As in drugs? There are drugs here? Are you serious? Omigod, omigod, omigod!"

My vivid imagination runs wild, adding up all the possible things that could go wrong. My restless hands fly up to my face, grab my frizzy hair, and tug once. My mouth drops open in a silent squeak, and when I go to take my hands down, my watch tangles in my 'fro. "Damn it!" Twisting and tugging makes it worse, and soon my hand is plastered against my head at a weird angle, palm out.

A group of guys walks by and one of them high-fives me. "Awesome get-up. Sticky chicks are hot." He grins, sweeping his eyes up and down my sweaty body, totally checking me out, before walking on. "Later babe, me and you." He makes a pair of guns with his fingers and clicks his tongue.

With my hand stuck to my head, I whine, "Erin." Her name has five syllables by the time I say the whole thing. She laughs and walks over to untangle my watch from my hair. "What's a sticky chick?"

"He means you have a rod up your ass." I gape at her and she gives me a look that says he's right. "Please, your middle name is Uptight. So is your first name, your last name, your Confirmation name, and your married name seems to be going that direction, too. Well done, Sticky Chick."

"I'm not uptight. I'm just careful. There's a difference. Like drugs here—bad move."

Erin laughs and shoves her dark hair out of her face. "Princess, I think some serious bubble-bursting is in order here. This is a rave. There is probably lots of stuff going on here tonight. But don't worry; things always go smoothly with these guys. There's security all over the place and by tomorrow, there will be no trace to prove that anything has ever happened here. See? Everything is hunky dory! Oh, I'd stay away from the restroom for the next little while if I were you. They've been fishbowling in there." She shrugs her shoulders as if I'm supposed to understand what she just said.

"Fishbowling?" Am I even supposed to know what that means?

"Yeah. You know, smoking weed in a small room to keep in the fumes? Unless you want to get high, then go right ahead. Free buzz. I just didn't think you'd be into that stuff." She says this as if we were at a

Sunday brunch with the local church ladies, exchanging scone recipes. This is an illegal rave in an old abandoned warehouse—and it was my idea. What the hell was I thinking? I'm going straight to Hell for this. I place my hands on my churning stomach... okay, so I'll go to Hell right after I throw up, but not in the restroom! Maybe I should start practicing pole dancing as well, just in case I have to resort to stripping for a living when my parents disown me. Gina is a good stripper nickname, right? My father is so going to shoot me. Oh, God!

"Why did I agree to this in the first place, Erin? And who are these people? It was supposed to be invite-only for a select and elite group of people. That's what we agreed on, but I don't know anyone here, and I'm part of the elite!" I'm poking at my chest so hard I've probably bruised a boob. Seriously! Who are these people? I've hobnobbed with the rich and pompous my entire life, and I've never seen any of these people before.

Erin stops her gyrating and takes me by the shoulders, looking straight in my eyes. I'm in full freak-out mode and she's trying to keep me in one piece. Normally, I'd appreciate the gesture on her part, but she's the reason I'm in this state. Someone who knows someone who knows Erin's downstairs neighbor asked Erin if she knew of anyone in the upper class community with an available space for a highly exclusive and swanky party, aka illegal rich-kid rave. Apparently, raves are back in style, and my bestie immediately thought of my Dad's old textile warehouse.

I'm a felon now.

ME!

Erin sighs dramatically. I can't really hear it, but I see her body cues and those flying, glowing hands clue me in. "You agreed, because even you want to get rid of that broomstick that's been shoved up your prissy ass! As for not knowing who these people are, well, you've been hanging out with the good kids all your life. This," she gestures grandly toward the entire room and its glow stick waving occupants, "is the fun crowd. Loosen up and let go! Dance. You love dancing!"

She pats my head like I'm a toddler, laughs and moves further into the swarm, attracting the attention of two guys who happily agree to be her dance partners. It's a sexy wiggly man sandwich with extra Erin in the middle.

UNEXPECTED VOYEUR

7:58 pm

I'm almost tempted to lose myself to the beat of the music—almost. Dancing would be a most welcome distraction right about now. If this had been any other party, I would have gladly joined in, but I can't dance here. I'm too afraid we'll be busted. As it is, I'm constantly looking through the windows and toward the door.

Erin is right, though. I have to learn to loosen up a little bit. This is just a party, and tomorrow it will be like nothing ever happened. I suck in a deep breath and release it, trying to slow my pulse into non-stroke territory.

Looking around, the place isn't recognizable. It actually looks like a swanky dance club, instead of a warehouse. The atmosphere is electric, and the live DJ keeps everyone in a trance with provocative, dark, scratchy and somewhat aggressive electro house and dubstep beats. The deep bass is making my chest vibrate with every pulse. Strobe lights flash in time, accompanied by a dizzying display of multicolored lasers under black lighting. These people are supposed to be the best in the business and I can see why. Everything looks and feels awesome. The party is a sensory experience in every way possible. No expense was spared on the set up, and the steep cover charge didn't keep people away either—not at this kind of party. It's the type of party everyone hopes to attend, but only the super awesome elite can succeed.

Since I just said super awesome elite, I'm obviously not one of them. I hang with a different crowd, save Erin. She's my lifeline, my reminder that life isn't all business and no fun. Her life is all fun. I can see her glowing arms wedged between two guys as they get swept away in the dense crowd.

Standing alone, I glance around. Elaborate wrought iron candleholders are on every available surface and deep red drapes have been hung, adding a bit of an eerie gothic, vampire-esque feel to the old warehouse. The final effect is kind of cool, actually. There are people everywhere, in every inch of the wide-open space. We're in violation of too many codes to count. As if that's the worst of my problems.

As my eyes scan the room, they lock on a couple partly hidden by stacks of old crates. I shift to get a better look, worried that I may need to call security if she's being assaulted. Of course my mind jumps to the worst-case scenario, but maybe I'm wrong.

As I take a few steps to the side to get a better view, it's clear that they are making out and it's getting hot and heavy. I should look away, give them their privacy, but there's just something in the way he's holding her that keeps me staring. It's possessive, rough and... erotic. I feel my cheeks getting hotter, which is saying something since this place already feels like a sauna, but I can't tear my eyes away. My lips part and I stare unabashedly. I can't help it.

She's pressed up against the wall, a leg wrapped around the guy's jean-clad hips. He's holding her wrists firmly above her head with one hand, the other hand pressed against the wall next to her head. His hips move to the beat of the music, pressing against her subtly and rhythmically. I continue to watch, unable to look away, as people around me keep on dancing, entwined in each other. Everyone here has that audacious thing going on, like a sexy train wreck about to happen, but not like this couple. I feel like such a creeper, but I can't seem to turn my head or blink. The man's shoulders are broad and you can tell through his tight black t-shirt that he's all toned muscle—and not the bulky kind, like on those cans of man-in-a-can. This guy is strong, with the perfect amount of muscle to accentuate his masculinity. I suppose the way he's holding her does that too, because damn…

Her head is tilted to the side, her long red curls cascading down the wall, her neck exposed for him to devour. Kudos to the party masters and their vampire theme; this couple fits right in.

Red's eyes are closed, her mouth wide open, as if she's gasping. She doesn't look like she's struggling or in any kind of distress. No, she's a very willing participant. My breath quickens and I start to feel warm in places I shouldn't. I'm enveloped in an overload of sensuality, from the music to the heat coming off of the bodies around me. Add in the passion of the couple in the dark and my heart is racing rapidly.

My fingers idly play with my short pearl necklace and I wonder what it would be like to be taken like that, so public and carnal. There's nothing romantic or loving about their embrace. It's raw, it's sexual, it's erotic.

It's like nothing I've ever experienced before, that's for sure. I wish I could see the look on his face. From my viewpoint, the way he moves, the way he's holding her, it's so possessive.

My thoughts are interrupted by a hip bump. A sticky plastic glass of some sickeningly sweet cocktail is being placed in my hand. It's Erin and she's out of breath, flushed, and giggling like crazy. Something tells me that it's not helium in those little balloons that I've seen people sucking on all night. Is laughing gas even legal?

"Here, drink up! What are we looking at?" Erin glances in the direction I'd been staring at just moments ago, still giggling.

A little embarrassed by my sudden case of voyeurism, I shrug, trying to look unaffected. "Just a couple making out, dry-humping in the corner over there, nothing much." I feel Erin's eyes boring into the side of my head. Bringing the glass to my mouth, I chug back half of its contents, not entirely registering how sweet and fruity it is, but knowing I should go slow. I'm a lightweight and this will go straight to my head, but I need to numb myself out just a little bit.

"Uhmmm, they're not dry-humping."

PUBLIC EXPOSURE

8:12 pm

"Nope, Gina. No dry-hump there." Erin squints her eyes to focus on the show a bit more. "He is most definitely hammering her straight into that wall. She'll be a permanent fixture by the time he's done. You pervy peeping tom, you!" Erin laughs a bit too loud. I cringe, wishing that I could crawl under a table and die.

A girl walks past us, staring at Erin and me. She's dressed like slutty Rainbow Brite, wearing a multicolored wig with a rainbow-colored ruffled bikini. Add in the rainbow furry leg warmers and tutu, complete with blinking lights, and she's the prism princess in the flesh.

Rainbow Bright looks at us with that happy dazed look on her face, the kind that comes from using illicit substances, and walks away after having thoroughly checked me out.

Shaking my head, I glance back toward the couple in the dark and see details I hadn't noticed before, like the way her skirt is hiked up to her hips and the way his black jeans seem to be unfastened, his belt hanging down a bit. Since neither one of them is glowing, I didn't notice before. Their bodies are mostly in shadow, but this is a warehouse with no private places to steal a kiss—or nail a woman to the wall.

The guy's movements are getting faster and more rough, his perfectly shaped ass clenching as he pushes against her again and again and again.

I have to look away. But I can't.

Erin laughs beside me. "Oh, my God! The look on your face is priceless! Don't tell me you're still a virgin? I thought Doctor Goody Two Shoes took care of that situation for you! " I tear my eyes away from the couple just long enough to look at my friend, her eyes almost popping out of her head in disbelief.

"No, I'm not a virgin. It's just. God, Erin! They're having sex in public! On the wall!" And it's hot and part of me wants some of that, too, which scares the tar out of me. But I can't say that out loud, because that would mean it's true. If I keep these little thoughts in my head, no one will ever know. They can't become real if no one knows about them. Can they?

Erin laces her arm over my shoulder and leans in. "So, you've never had any public hanky-panky before? Not even a little fingering under the table, or a bathroom stall blowjob, or going downtown on your man in the car?" Erin asks waggling her eyebrows before I shake her off.

"No!" I shake my head, as if the idea were repulsive, not sure why I'm so defensive.

I haven't done anything like that. Ever. In bed, my boyfriend is more the slow and sweet type. Anthony is nothing like this. My eyes go back to the couple. His pace is picking up even more. What they are doing is now unmistakable. The girl is biting her lip, probably to stifle a scream, and I can't help but mimic her expression. The spot down low in the pit of my stomach stirs, and my grip tightens around my glass. She throws her head back and, when he finally stills, his body pressed to hers, she sags, dropping her head on his shoulder. They are both breathing heavily. I'm almost panting along with them.

What would it feel like to be her? To be held up against a wall like that, and be taken so roughly, without any inhibitions?

My inner-voice chides me, "Stop it, Gina. That might work for some people, but not you."

Once more, Erin interrupts my lusty daydreams. "Go Ferro. You sexy beast! Grrrrr!" She claws at the air as if she were a bear.

"Ferro? They're here? Where? I didn't see any of them walk in." On my tiptoes, I look around the mass of bodies, trying to find anyone in the crowd that would fit their trademark description.

The Ferro family is one of the oldest

and richest families in New York. Hell, they're the wealthiest family in the Tri-State Area. My family is pretty well off, and from what is called "old money", which is another way to say "my ancestors worked their butts off to make it big and we're keeping the ball rolling", but the Ferros are insanely rich, powerful... and scary.

It is wise to never ask a Ferro for a favor, because you never want to be in their debt. On the other hand, if they ask a favor of you, you NEVER refuse. You don't want to be on Constance Ferro's shit list. She's head of the Ferro clan, and a very imposing woman, to put it mildly. I've met her and her husband on various occasions, mostly during fundraisers and social functions. Her three sons, on the other hand, I have yet to meet, although they constantly make their way to the social pages of the paper every time one of them screws up. It seems like not a day goes by without one of the Ferro boys making headlines.

"Uh, yeah Gina. That would be Mr. Humpty Dumped-His-Load over there. You didn't recognize him?" I shake my head.

Erin huffs in exasperation. "Regina

Granz! Where have you been the past couple of years? That hot guy nailing the redhead to the wall is Pete Ferro."

THE SEXY BEAST

8:33 pm

"I never thought I'd actually see the sex god in action!" Erin makes a high pitched squeal only dogs or dolphins could hear, and balances on the balls of her feet, trying to get a better view. "I can die a happy girl now. Best. Party. Ever, Gina!" Erin lets out a contented sigh before dramatically falling sideways onto my shoulder. I have no idea what expression is on my face, but Erin laughs and kisses me on the cheek before heading back toward the crowd.

"Stop kissing me!" I yell after her,

wiping away her lipstick. It's not until I yell the words that I realize what I've said. My cheeks warm, and I back away from the few faces that reassess me. Erin's answering giggles are swallowed by the noise of the crowd.

That's when a whirl of red hair catches my eye. It's not my fault. I swear I'm not a perv, but they're in my line of sight now. I stare at the couple, wondering things that shouldn't be thought, clutching a crumpled plastic cup in one hand and my cell in the other.

Did I really just imagine what it would feel like to have sex with—eck—Pete Ferro?

Where's my mental Lysol? That's so gross. Of all people, I swoon over the most notorious asshat. It's a well-known fact that he sleeps with every woman he comes into contact with and punches whatever guy gets in his way. Just the thought of him would make any respectable girl like myself slap on a chastity belt, throw away the key, and run for the hills. Guys like him can't be trusted. They're all smiles and sweet-talk until the panties drop. When the conquest is over, they're gone. From what I've heard about

Pete, Red is going to be old news as soon as he zips his fly.

With my eyes still on Pete and his newest conquest, I watch them straighten their clothing. He turns around and that's when I recognize him—the dark messy hair, the shocking blue eyes, and the cocky self-satisfactory grin on his stubbly face. Damn. He's hotter than I thought. The way the light falls across his face makes him look like an angel, freshly fallen. Shadows play across his eyes, making him look like he should be the Wikipedia entry for SINFUL. The pictures I've seen of him in the tabloids and gossip columns are lacking. They don't reveal that combustible aura about him, like his errant glance could cause you to erupt in flames at any second. He's male perfection on the outside, from his freshly fucked hair down to his tight firm butt in those slim-fitting jeans. Too bad he's an asshole.

Pete's lazy gaze scans the room and connects with mine just as my eyes drift past his hips. My spine goes ramrod straight and my stomach flips. Oh crap! He's looking straight at me. He holds my gaze, offering a crooked grin that becomes devilish.

I gulp and force my gaping mouth shut. He knows I've been watching. He knows I saw everything. That look, the way he devours me with his eyes, makes my palms sweat and fires up parts of me I wish it wouldn't. Pete scans my body up and down, as if I'm his next meal. I feel naked, despite my clothes. My insides quiver and I let out a shaky breath. He's trying to rattle me, but I refuse to let him. My gaze remains on him, eyes narrowed, and obviously not interested.

At least not interested in him. The concept of being desired like that is what caught my attention. The fact that the man is Pete Ferro makes me wish I followed Erin into the crowd. Besides, a guy like that isn't serious. He's a one-off, a fling. I want steady and I found a steady guy. He's the most brilliant up-and-coming doctor on the East Coast. But while I'm proud of him, while he's everything I wanted, I've never been with him like that. Passion isn't something we do. So when Pete checks me out, my heart stops. I'm the polar opposite of the woman in his arms. Why is he even looking at me?

That's when Pete winks and throws his head to the side slightly, an invitation to join them.

Not him, THEM.

My thoughts shatter, clanging on the floor like a dropped gong. Every single piece of my previous lust—or whatever that was—drops into my shoes. Blinking twice, I stiffen as my jaw flaps open. Heat flashes through me, streaking across my face and over my chest, and pooling in my belly. I ignore that last part.

I just, I can't even... Is he really inviting me over for a threesome? Who does that?

Disgusted, and slightly mortified, I look away. Damn it! We were in a visual tug-of-war and I lost. I slap my mouth shut and push my way through the crowd. Sweaty bodies bump into me, and there's an occasional pair of hands that grabs hold of my hips before I manage to break away. I may have growled at one guy, who immediately released me. I suspect Pete would have held on tighter. Freak.

My stomach is still in a suspended motion, like I'm walking on Mars. Wrapping my arms around my middle, I tighten my grip on my phone and keep my eyes glued to the floor. Although I'm in a mass of people, I can still feel eyes on me. My fingers straighten and ball up again as I think about it. What a jerk. I know he just did that to get to me. No one would ever invite me to a threesome. I mean, look at me. I'm the only woman here who isn't flashing boob every two seconds. Mine are wrapped up tightly in my virginal little blouse. So again, why would he ask me to be part of a sex sandwich? Do I look like that's my thing? Maybe he thought my pearl necklace was made of butt beads.

Scowling, I shoulder my way through the crowd, putting as much distance as possible between Pete Ferro and me. The music continues to pulse and I wish I could relax, but that's not my MO. I'm uptight Gina, the chick with the pearls around her throat, not up her ass. The stick is in the way.

My shoulders sag as I stop and back up to lean against a wall. Why do I even care? So what if Pete Ferro thinks I'm a prude? Who cares if he was teasing me or serious? It doesn't matter. For one, I'm dating someone, and reason number next—he's Pete Ferro—and it's been confirmed that the tabloids didn't make the man. He did that himself by nailing women to the wall with his thingy, in public!

I shiver thinking about it. I can't even kiss in public. When I feel other eyes on me I freeze. The action lacks intimacy and seems wrong.

Laughing to myself, I think, maybe I am a prude.

THE GOOD GUY

8:47 pm

Just then, my cell phone vibrates, flashing my boyfriend's name across the little screen. I love him but crap! Anthony can't know what's going on here tonight, he'll blab to Dad about it. Since Anthony's working the night shift in the ER for his residency in med school, the timing for this party was perfect. He's probably just on his break and calling to say goodnight and a quick I love you.

I'm not a total ass; I would have invited him. The thing is I needed to unwind and have some time with Erin. Then my girl time turned into this. A rave with drugs and half-naked women isn't really his scene. Too many people in too small a space, plus the added opportunity of going to jail, not finishing his degree, and alienating himself from his future seemed like unnecessary temptation. So I didn't give him the option. I feel a little bad about that, about being here without him. Maybe I should go.

The phone continues ringing in my hand, as I gaze across the warehouse and the throng of people, tables, and dancers between the door and me. I'll talk to him and then bail. Erin can have enough fun for two people. This isn't my scene.

Headed toward a spot where the noise level is at a minimum, I run up an old metal staircase toward the storage room. After a couple forceful pushes and tugs on the handle, I notice that the lock at the bottom of the door is on. It's the kind that slides down into a hole in the floor. Lifting the pin with my foot, I slip the lock up, and push the door open.

I might be a little bit tipsy from having chugged down my drink so fast. I'm also frustrated with the way this whole evening is turning out, and the fact that I'm still irritated over a Ferro. I slam the door shut and take a deep breath before answering the phone. Luckily for me, the room is more soundproof than I remembered. The bass is just a dull vibration on the floor, and the walls and the door muffle most of the high-pitched treble sounds.

"Hey, babe," I say, answering the call.

"Where are you? The phone rang forever. I thought you fell down a well or something," Anthony teases. I think of myself as graceful, I mean who ever heard of a clumsy dancer? But Anthony has this way of making me feel awkward.

I laugh it off. "Ha, ha. I'm fine. Just hanging out with Erin."

He groans. "Oh God, seriously? I thought it was bath night?"

The way he says it makes me sound like an old lady with too many cats. My brows pinch together. "It might be, and Erin's not that bad."

"Fine, whatever. It's just that she always gets you into trouble, and then where…" Static cuts through the line and his voice fades in and out. I have no idea what he's saying, but I know he's still mad about Erin.

I interrupt. "You're breaking up. I can't hear you."

He tries to answer, "Babe...they... come," and then more static.

"Anthony, you're breaking up." My phone beeps, making me look down at the screen. The battery flashes two percent. Aw, crap. Pressing it to my ear I hear him still trying to talk. "I can't hear you. Don't worry. I'm heading home, okay? The night was completely uneventful. A bust." Lots of busts—in fact, it was boobfest of the year. I smirk and wish I could joke with him like that, but he'll think I'm being crass.

"All right, well, I just wanted to tell you goodnight. Who loves you?"

I smile like a dork. "You do."

"Who's my good girl?"

"I am." I roll my eyes at this little ritual. Anthony started it almost as soon as we met. If he were here, he'd kiss my cheek and pat my head. Other women might take that wrong, but he means well. "I love you. Don't stay too late."

"I won't be by in the morning. Sorry

babe, work has been crazy. If I don't get my shut-eye, I'm no good to anyone. I promise I'll…and then…" his voice breaks as more static sizzles in my ear. He keeps talking even though my battery is beeping. I keep trying to tell him that the phone is going dead.

"Anthony—"

"This patient was really…" he keeps talking, like he can't hear me at all.

"Hey, my phone is—" Too late. It cuts him off mid-sentence and the screen goes black. Totally dead. Great. Looks like I'll have to hail a cab. So much for the catch-a-cab app.

I tuck my phone in the back pocket of my jeans and pad back toward the door. I pull on the handle and give it a big tug. It doesn't move. The thing was sticking on the way in, so I yank again, throwing my whole body into the tug this time, but it doesn't budge. My stomach drops.

"No. Nononononono! This can't be happening!" Making sure the handle is turned properly, I pull on the door again but it still won't move.

My heart starts to pound at the

frightening prospect of being locked in. I try to wiggle and jiggle the door some more, playing with the handle as much as I can, but my hands are getting sweaty and slipping. The door seems to be jammed from the bottom.

Oh, no. The facts hit me hard and fast, I must have slammed the door too hard when I came in and the metal pin slid back down into its hole in the floor. Banging my forehead on the door with a painful thump, I exhale loudly. This evening is just clusterfucktabulous.

What else could go wrong? Feeling my cell phone press into my butt from the rear pocket of my jeans, I get the answer to what was supposed to be a rhetorical question.

Damn it. I forgot that my battery is dead.

I can't call anyone for help.

Worst.

Party.

Ever.

KARMA IS A MEGA-BITCH

9:02 pm

"HEY!" I scream repeatedly at the top of my lungs, but the only response is the echo of the empty room.

Pressing my forehead to the door, I curse myself for stepping over that pristine line I was taught to follow. Mother made it crystal clear that following the rules would make me happy. The one time I deviate, I get locked in a storage room. Karma is a mega-bitch.

The music is blaring downstairs and although I doubt anyone can hear me, I start bellowing again. The thought of being locked in here when everyone leaves makes my skin crawl. Alone in an abandoned warehouse—no, bad plan. The thought of falling asleep on the floor and waking up to a rat gnawing on my face flashes in my mind. Goosebumps break out up and down my arms and I pound harder on the door.

"HELP! IS ANYONE THERE?" My throat is on fire and my fists feel like they've been through a trash compactor. Slapping a metal door hurts. My skin stings a little more each time it impacts the cold rough surface of the door.

Then it dawns on me: Erin is the only person who knows I'm here. Once the crew strikes the decorations and the DJ takes off, no one will ever mention it again. It's not like people brag about being at an illegal party. They're smarter than that. There will be no evidence to prove a rave took place here tonight, save the girl trapped in the upstairs storage room. That's the moment my world tips on its axis, and logic slides away like pudding off a plate. Panic, raw and real, takes its place. A shiver climbs up my spine and tightens my throat. Heart pounding, I slam my fists against the door, wildly banging on it, trying to make as much noise as possible.

"HELP! SOMEONE LET ME OUT! HELP! PLEASE! I'M IN HERE! HELP! " Repeating variations of the same words over and over and over again, I continue to yell and bang on the metal. I continue to bang on and kick at the door, yelling for help even though the inner rational part of me recognizes it's pointless. This room is so far away from the crowd, and the music coming from downstairs is so loud, there is no way anyone can hear me. I know this, but fear takes over, and I keep screaming until my voice is hoarse and my fists are too sore to take another hit.

Throat raw and hands aching, I finally slump down onto the ground, defeated, my back resting against the door. Tears spill over and roll down my cheeks. Every loud sob feels like a handful of sand making its way down my throat, it's gritty and hurts like hell.

I hate being weak, but I hate being stuck in this small, dirty and stuffy storage room even more. Who knows how long it will take before I am found? The thought is terrifying. I could be stuck in here for days. How long can someone survive, without food or water, in such a small space?

Tugging my collar, I shift a little. The air is stagnant and warmer than before, or it seems that way. My hand moves nervously to my necklace and my fingers start to roll the small pearls.

I hope it doesn't take Erin too long to notice I've gone missing, but I'm not counting on it. She's probably in the middle of a sexcapade. I pull my legs up to my chest, wrap my arms around my ankles, and rest my head on my knees.

Sometimes I wish I were more like Erin. She's a free spirit, flighty at best, always living in the moment. If I'm not in her face, I don't exist—out of sight, out of mind. Anthony is so busy with med school we sometimes go days without talking. Even though he said he was going home to sleep, it wouldn't be unusual for him to work a double instead. My parents won't even notice if I'm gone for a few days, being preoccupied with our family's business. My dead phone won't alarm anyone, because it's something that's been happening a lot lately. I dropped the damn thing and it won't hold a charge for more than a few hours. If I'd found time to buy a new battery, I wouldn't be in this mess. I could just call Erin to open the door.

There is no one else. I've always been too shy to stand out. I have a few close friends and that's it. If I stood out, if I was the life of the party—or hell, if I said yes to Ferro—someone would have noticed I went missing. No one will even notice I'm gone.

I'm so screwed.

NO TIME FOR REGRETS

10:23 pm

In my panic, my mind begins to play tricks on me. The walls appear to be closing in and it's getting harder to breathe, like I'm running out of air. It's just in my head, but it doesn't stop a bead of sweat from rolling down my temple. I sigh and rest my cheek on my knees, then rock back and forth, gently.

My next logical plan, my last hope, is to just sit here and wait until the music stops and then resume my noisy attempt at being discovered when the cleanup crew packs everything up. Maybe a pair of horny partygoers looking for a secluded place for a quick tryst will come by and open the door. One can only hope. With my shit-for-luck, it'll be Ferro with another random floozy.

I don't know how long I've been sitting here, rocking back and forth, but the music stops abruptly, mid-song. It can't be the end of the party already. There must be some technical glitch with the sound system. Cocking my ear toward the door I listen and wait, but the music doesn't start up again. A surge of hope fills me. This is my chance. With the music off, I need to be as loud as I can. They have to hear me.

Jumping up, I bang on the metal door. As soon as my hand connects with the metal I scream, or croak. My voice is gone. I'm making horrible troll sounds, as if a goat wandered onto my bridge. Cradling my hand against my chest, I freeze.

I can hear people, but it's not the type of party noise I heard before. A chill races up my spine and I press my ear to the door trying to hear better.

Through the thick metal, I hear cries that chill me to the bone. People are yelling, not insults or profanity, but the blood curdling screams of panic and fear. Something horribly wrong is going on down there. Oh, God. I press my hand to my chest and step away from the door, wide-eyed.

Visions of a mass murderer wearing a hockey mask and waving a chainsaw pop through my mind. But that's just ludicrous. There were no gunshots. If I could hear the music, I should have heard if someone went nuts and shot the place up. No, it's something else. Something worse.

Frantic, I look around, trying to find something that I can use to pound on the door, but there's nothing but a few boxes of paper filled with old receipts. As the screaming from downstairs increases, my blood races faster through my veins. I can hear my heart pounding in my ears.

If people are screaming—if something is that wrong—the cops will come. If the cops come here then I'm toast. I'll get my ass thrown in jail for hosting a rave here, and Daddy will get hit with a ton of fines. Worse still, they could toss him in jail, too. Cupping my hands to my face I take a shaky breath and try to hold it together. I did this. Whatever happens is my fault, and I'll take the blame. They aren't going to pin this on Daddy or anyone else.

Pressing my back to the wall, I slide back down to the floor. At least they'll find me before a rat makes me his bitch. At least things can't get worse. Just as I think it, I push my hair out of my face and notice it's damp because I'm sweating like crazy. God this room is hot.

As I stare at the ceiling I talk into the air, "God, if you get me out of this I'll go back to being a good girl. I promise." I'm hoping there's not a stampede downstairs. If someone gets hurt, I won't be able to live with myself. Sitting here is driving me nuts and I've sweat through my shirt. I need to get out of here so I can help. Tipping my head back against the wall, I look up. "Give me a sign, what do I do?"

As if in answer, the sprinkler in the ceiling above me goes off and rains down on my face, as the blaring of the fire alarm deafens me. Great! Now someone pulled the alarm. More fines. I'm so going to jail for this. Daddy is going to kill me. When I lower my face, I blink twice and try to wipe the water away from my eyes. I sniff the air and then do it again. No. It can't be.

Is that smoke? Black puffs seep under the crack in the door. I laugh bitterly and stare at the door with my jaw hanging open. It wasn't a false alarm. It's real. The building is on fire. That's why they're screaming. That's why I'm so hot and something is burning my throat when I breathe. I thought it was from yelling, but that's not it. I'm inhaling burnt air filled with chemicals from downstairs. The little light overhead flickers and dies, leaving me in darkness.

For a moment, I freeze and the world stops. Fight or die. Get that door open Gina or you won't see another sunrise.

Jumping up, I race to the door and pound wildly as I scream. The tiny room is filling up with smoke swiftly and turning into an oven. Black clouds billow from under the door and through the vents in the floor. I feel them filling the room as it becomes hotter and hotter. Vapors burn as I desperately try to gulp the air, but I can't. It burns my nostrils and lungs making me scream out.

Bending over, I choke, unable to stop. I claw at my throat and feel panic overtaking me. My hands are around my neck as my knees give out. As I fall to the floor, I hear something snap. My tiny fresh-water pearls scatter.

I can't die like this. Not now. Not here.

Crawling toward the door, I feel for the hinges and dig my nails in trying to pry them off of the wall. My nails snap and my fingers ache as I try to force them to do something they weren't made to do. I try one last time to get some leverage, to feel for a weak spot on the frame of the door, but there's nothing—no way out.

The smoke keeps coming. I try to hold my breath, but I can't. I gasp, inhaling a dangerous amount of the toxins before doubling over with a fit of coughing and try to catch my breath. My skin is slick with sweat and I'm too hot. My head is getting that weird spacey feeling, and it feels like the floor is tipping sideways.

Lowering my body, I press my cheek to the old wooden floorboards. It's not until I feel a sharp stabbing sensation that I realize I'm clawing the ground. Splinters lodge in my nail beds as tears mix with water and run down my cheeks.

I wasted it. My life is over and I wasted the whole thing.

THE LAST DANCE

11:17 pm

The one time I break the rules, I go down in flames, literally. The little storage room is so hot, I feel like I'm being cooked alive. The air won't go down my throat and every time I try, it feels like trying to breathe through plastic wrap. Tears streak my warm face, rolling off my cheeks, and onto the wooden floor. I watch it darken for a moment, and then the ring of tears shrinks until another takes its place.

This was all for nothing. My entire life amounted to nothing. I wasn't kind. I didn't help anyone. There's no reason for anyone to remember me. My life will be reduced to a pile of credit cards and a social security number. My name is worthless—no one will remember Regina Granz.

The thing is, I thought I'd have more time. More time to be brave, to be bold, to be daring, to become whoever I was supposed to be. While I waited for that girl to show up, I fell in line, doing as I was told, never asking why...never speaking out. I was so focused on what everyone else wanted for me that I never asked what I wanted.

Now it's too late.

I've found the spot on the floor with the coolest air. There must be a crack in the exterior, because a tiny wisp of blissfully cool air meets me now and then. It's no bigger than a thread, but it's there. On the other side of this wall is fresh air and freedom.

I make promises to myself, and then finally to a deity I rarely talk to. I don't know if He's here or not, but if there is a God then He can hear my thoughts, my pleas. I'll do something with my life if you spare me.

I promise.

I won't be the self-absorbed, overly cautious Gina I've been for so long. I'll make a difference; I've always wanted to, I just didn't know how.

I manage to roll onto my back and I turn my head toward the ceiling, letting the water from the sprinkler above fall down on my face like rain. It's eerily soothing. My limbs turn to lead and I struggle to keep my eyelids open. Smoke lingers above me. I know it's there, even if I can't see it. The swirling heat is getting closer, filling the tall room from the ceiling, creeping toward the floor.

My fear is gone, leaving my imagination to run wild with an unending parade of wishes and regrets. I dig my fingernails into the floorboards, trying to stay awake, but I feel the heaviness upon me, pulling me under. I fight it, letting the pain from broken nails and old splinters stab a sharp sensation up my arms.

Pictures flicker like an old movie behind my eyelids, until my mind wanders to the one thing that has always brought me solace —dancing. The ghosts of past performances play through my mind. Every step, every controlled movement, the raw pain from dancing on point for hours on end, toes blistered and bleeding, and loving every excruciating minute of it.

I focus my mind on a single routine, forcing myself to be in the dance and not in the burning storage room. I feel pride in the control I have over my body, as I move into perfect lines and curves. I feel my muscles pull into each position, the way they stretch and move, strong and sure. I feel each spin, lunge, and leap, sparing me from the regret crushing my chest. The moves are vivid in my mind and overpower my fear of dying, my lost dreams. I push back my sadness, knowing I won't say goodbye to my mom and my daddy. Each mental movement hides the despair swimming in my stomach because I couldn't breach the barrier keeping me from safety. Each mental movement conceals the disappointment that consumes me most—that my life was meaningless, I did nothing, achieved nothing.

Confusion obliterates reality and I feel it slip from my grasp like a fallen rose petal. In my mind I continue dancing, turning, and feeling the strength of my body—strength that is gone. This is my last dance. Giselle dies of a broken heart in her lover's arms. Stage lights flash in my eyes, blinding me so there is nothing, no one out there. The audience is a mass of black, fading until there is nothing left except me and the wooden floor of a smoke covered stage. My fingers release from the planks, and my hand lifts enough to finish the scene.

But the dance isn't over. Giselle's lover discovers her lifeless body and the dance continues. His body is strong and sure, but I do not dance. These legs will not move. Sleep calls me in a thick deep voice, over and over again.

A distraught man, Giselle's lover, lifts me up and cradles my dead body in his arms. With one hand around his neck and the other, on his shoulder, I rest my head on his strong chest and sigh one last time. This is my final bow. The curtain falls and plunges me into darkness like I've never known.

TAKE ME AWAY

11:59 pm

Darkness surrounds me. My body feels sluggish, like it's stuck in cement. I want to hold on to the comfortable lethargy that envelops me, but it's slowly dissipating against my will. I'm being rocked, back and forth, as if on a sailboat across the waves, with an intensely warm breeze blowing across my face. The rhythmic movement is calming. I must have fallen asleep on our sailboat, anchored somewhere along the coast of St. Lucia. Did Daddy take Mom and me to the Caribbean? I can't remember.

I'm vaguely aware of my damp clothing sticking to my skin.

Confusing images swirl through my mind. They morph and change, blending in and out of each other like in a dream. I see pictures of people laughing, neon colors being waved around, candles everywhere, fluffy leg warmers, people kissing in dark corners, a skintight black shirt with midnight blue eyes, and smoke.

Smoke. The fire.

Feeling panic crawl up my spine in a swift wave. There's a fire. I'm trapped. I try to open my eyes, but they sting too much and immediately shut tight again. Forcing my eyes open again, I blink repeatedly. A blurry image slowly comes into focus through a watery film. Trying to piece all the information together doesn't work. My brain moves in slow motion and I don't understand. The smoke that filled my nostrils is gone and I feel soft fabric beneath my cheek—no wooden planks. Delirium has overtaken me. I'm hallucinating; I must be, because I seem to be in some guy's arms.

Am I dead? Is this the Grim Reaper? I

thought he was supposed to be scary, but I'm not getting that vibe from this guy. He's not a firefighter—no mask or costume. Wait, not a costume, what's that called?

My head hurts, and thinking is making it worse. I try to take things at face value, or at least what seems most likely. I'm pretty sure my body is still burning in the building. I died and a beautiful death angel is looking at me with beautiful, heavenly eyes. I blink again, slowly trying to focus. The guy holding me is drop dead, smoking hot—no pun intended—gorgeous. I sigh contentedly and snuggle into him, as he holds me close to his chest. The rocking movement slows down gradually to a stop.

"Hey. You're awake." His rich voice rushes out in relief and concern, and the way his lips lightly turn up into a small smile makes my mind turn to jelly. Oh, wow! I know I should respond, say something, anything, but I can't. The connection between my brain and my mouth seems to be malfunctioning.

"Do you think you can stand?" Sexy Reaper guy asks with the best bedroom voice I've ever heard. Is it bad to think of him and bedrooms in the same thought? Goosebumps tingle all over, and with every coherent thought gone, all I can do is nod dumbly.

The words are right there, on the tip of my tongue, but he puts me down gently on my feet. Standing so very close beside me, he holds me in place, one arm around my waist, and one hand on one of my shoulders. As he loosens his grip and I try to stand on my own, I'm hit with the biggest headache known to man and I know in that instant, without a doubt, that I'm still very much alive.

Reality hits me in the face like a splintered two by four.

Fuck, that hurts! My head feels like it's going to explode. I'd take a hangover over this feeling any day. It feels like someone is scraping the inside of my skull with a fork. I desperately want to put both my hands on either side of my head and squeeze until my eyes pop out, but the world around me is spinning out of control. I sway, falling toward the ground, but, thankfully, I never make it to the cement. Sexy Reaper catches me, making sure I don't face plant.

My hands hit a wall of firm muscle, and excruciating pain shoots up my arms from my fingertips. I try to scream out in pain, but a horrible gritty squawk comes out instead. My voice is hoarse from my previous screaming and all the smoke. I sound like a dying dog. My throat and chest protest, and I'm assaulted with a bout of disgusting phlegmy coughing, making the pain in my head unbearable. I double over at the waist and I feel hands rubbing my back comfortingly until the coughing stops and I'm gasping for air. Ok, so no more screaming for a while.

"Whoa, steady there. Take it slow." The soothing voice helps to calm me and I try to breathe in the cool night air.

When I look up, I blink and stare at the person beside me. The man's beautiful face is covered with soot. Drops of water roll down from his dark wet hair, trailing down his cheeks, forming lines across the black patches on his cheeks and along his jaw. His blue eyes stand out like beacons, flashing in the dark night, conveying a look of apprehension.

Pete Ferro.

HELL FREEZES OVER

JUNE 29TH, 12:27 am

"It's you!" That's all I can manage to whisper, as mortification makes its way through my confusion.

The last time I saw him, he was packing his, uh, thingy into his pants and inviting me to join him and his date. A shadow of a smile lines his lips and a hint of a dimple threatens to surface. Oh, God! He remembers. His smirk is gone quickly and replaced by a frown. He tucks himself under one of my arms so that it's draped across his shoulders and places his hands on either side of my waist, offering me support.

"Listen to me. We have to get you some help. We'll straighten up very slowly. Ready?" Pete is all business and doesn't acknowledge my stupid-ass comment or the evening's embarrassing events.

It's you? Who the hell says that? Of course it's him! Who else would he be? Maybe he doesn't recognize me after all. I nod uncertainly, and he slowly helps to ease me back into an upright position.

As we slowly walk across the lot, I become more and more aware of my surroundings. The scene before me is utter chaos. I look around and see parked cars scattered everywhere, people running, hugging each other, the massive warehouse up in flames. The smell of the burning warehouse is sickening. The heat radiating from the inferno is scalding. Large columns of smoke swirl up toward the night sky, like a dreadful genie being released from an evil bottle. Horrified screams ring out, filling my ears as we walk. Emergency vehicles are rolling onto the scene, their lights flashing and their ear-splitting sirens drowning out all other sound.

It's a nightmare.

I collapse down to my knees, my shaky legs unable to keep me up any longer. The weight of reality is too much to bear. "What have I done?" My voice is barely a whisper, but at least I don't hack up a lung this time. Ashamed, I cover my face with my shaking hands to hide my tears. This is entirely my fault. All these people are in danger because of me. I look around, allowing the image of people huddled together screaming and crying, others running around frantically to be forever etched in my brain. I did this.

"Shhhh," Pete says softly while rubbing my back. "We're almost there, just a couple more steps. You can do this." Pete is crouching in front of me. He waits a second before prying my fingers from my face. He sees me flinch and examines my hands, frowning once more. I cough in between sobs, trying to catch my breath.

"Okay, that's it. We need to get you to the hospital now, that cough sounds really bad. Let me help you. Please." The pleading tone in his voice snaps me out of my guilt trip.

That's when I notice the ambulance nearby. That's where he is taking me. I pull back. The sudden motion makes me fall flat on my ass. I yank my hands away from Pete's grip, trying to crawl backwards, not caring that the motion makes my hands hurt worse than they already do.

I can't go to the hospital. I can't. I just...

Pete notices my sudden panic and looks directly at me, eyebrows pinched together. He places his hands on my shoulders, preventing me from escaping. I can't breathe. I'm going to jail for this. I'm sure of it. All I wanted was to feel like my life was my own, just for a moment. All my life I've been my father's daughter, my mother's perfect clone. I wanted to be me tonight, Gina, whoever she is. I start to hyperventilate, bringing on another fit of coughing.

"Hey, are you all right?" I have to shut my eyes when Pete asks.

I can't deal with the guilt of the things I've done. I can't tell him the truth, but I can't let him take me to them either. I shake my head. "I can't go to the EMTs. They'll take me to the hospital. I can't go there.

They'll know what I've done." I'm panicking, but I can't help it. I clasp my hands to my mouth, trying to control my breathing. This was not supposed to happen. No one was supposed to get hurt. No one was supposed to know. If I go to the hospital, Anthony is going to find out and he'll tell my father. They'll know that I was responsible for this. At best, I've burned down Daddy's building. At worst, there are still people inside—trapped like I was. Oh, God. My lip trembles, and I'm about to cry when Pete squeezes one of my shoulders.

"You need medical attention. Besides, it can't be all that bad. You get caught at an illegal party. So what? What's the worst that can happen? Daddy will take away the keys to your Mercedes?" When I open my eyes again, the look he gives me is too much. It's patronizing, like he's seen much worse and I'm freaking out for nothing. Hell, I know he's had more than one brush with the law. The man leaves a wake of destruction in his path, wherever he goes. Yet here he is, offering his help. He uses one hand to push my wet ratty hair out of my face. I really don't deserve any of this. I don't deserve his concern. He doesn't know what this means for me. The repercussions will be disastrous. It was only supposed to be a party.

I think back to all my regrets I'd felt while I was waiting to die in that storage room, how I'd wished I'd been more daring, how I'd wished for the opportunity to do the right thing. The honorable thing to do would be to go to the EMTs, have the truth come out, and suffer the consequences, but I can't let the evening's events be all for nothing. I need to claim my life for my own. I almost died tonight, and was given a second chance at life. I'm not throwing it away by going to jail.

Grabbing Pete's hand, I do the first thing that comes to mind. I need to call in a favor, and it just so happens that it's from a Ferro. Who knows, I may regret this later, but I don't care. I can't think that far ahead. I have to leave before the police get here and start taking people to the station for questioning. I ignore the pounding in my head, and the fuzzy dizziness threatening to throw me back down. I stand up and pull him away from the ambulance. It's time I finally take charge of my life. With a new sense of resolve, I look him in the eye.

"You don't understand. I need to leave now. No one can know I was here tonight, and it's more than what you think. Please. Will you help me? Take me away from here?"

RIDING A SEX GOD (I MEAN, RIDING NEXT TO A SEX GOD)

1:49 am

It must have been the way I said it, because he looks around, puts his hand on my back, and nods, convinced. With a more hurried stride, he leads me to the far end of the lot on the opposite side of the street. The parking spaces next to the building still hold a few cars trapped between the fire trucks and the building. The cost of the fire damage is going to be astronomical.

In the back of my mind I say a prayer,

begging God that everyone made it out alive. I've talked to God more tonight than in the past five years total. At the end, it seemed like the only thing that mattered. I thought I was toast, but this lunatic next to me ran through fire to pull me out.

Who does that? Is Pete an adrenaline junkie? I stop myself. I shouldn't judge. But the thought lingers in my mind, as my eyes trail up his trim frame. I should thank him, and stop acting like he has ulterior motives. The guy isn't a criminal, and he risked his life to save mine.

Pete's skin is covered in black soot and dotted with burns. He has a cut above his eyebrow and blood smeared all the way to his temple. His hair and clothes are damp. The fabric of his t-shirt clings to his body, moving with him as he walks, clinging to each muscle.

We stop at a sleek, black, two-seater vintage convertible, and he pulls a set of keys from his pocket. Pete opens up the passenger door, "Watch your head."

I see what he means. I duck to avoid the leather roof, and ease myself into the low, sporty convertible. My hands are so torn up from clawing the floor and the door of the storage room, putting on my seat belt is a challenge. I begin to think about being trapped in the storage room, and chills run up my spine. Pete yanks open his door and slips into the seat next to me, startling me out of the memory.

Inside and out, Pete's car looks like an early 1960's vintage sports car, but it has lots of new technology, too. I stare at the custom stereo, a thumb drive sticking out of one corner, and I wonder what kind of music he listens to. It says something about a person, but I don't ask. The clock flashes info at us, until Pete tells the car to stop talking to him.

The engine purrs to life, and, in a matter of moments, streetlights whip by. I stare out the window, resting my head against the cool glass. Although it leaves a sooty faceprint, it helps to alleviate the constant throbbing behind my skull. Better a faceprint, than an assprint. I giggle to myself, and wonder where that thought came from.

As Pete bobs and weaves through traffic, heading back onto Long Island, we sit in comfortable silence. The inky sky is perfect, save a spattering of stars. I stare at them, wondering if this is my last night of freedom. I deserve whatever happens to me. Hosting a rave was reckless. I know exactly what my father will say when he finds out, and I will deserve it. I just want a few more minutes to process everything and stop shaking. My hands won't stay still, even though I've tucked them in the crooks of my arms. It makes my nails throb, but pretty much everything makes them hurt.

Pete handles his car like he's been driving it his entire life. He's fast and reckless; if I wasn't in shock, I'd be screaming right now. He cuts across three lanes of traffic, and then darts through a just-turned-red light, before flooring it onto the expressway. He barely slows down to see if there's oncoming traffic.

As he shifts gears, his elbow bumps into mine. The jolt makes me pull my face off the glass and glance over at him. As soon as we're barreling down the expressway, he retrieves a cell phone from his back pocket. Pete fumbles with the screen and sets it down on the console in front of him.

The interior of his car is all brand new supple red leather. The dashboard has multiple circular chrome dials. The car swerves a little bit, as he gets the phone in place. I tense in my seat, trying not to grab the door. Erin hates it when I do that, even though she can't drive worth a damn. Well, that's not exactly true. She can drive into things, like shopping carts and the guardrail on the Sagtikos Parkway. How do you hit a parkway rail? It's not like they jump out and say BOO!

Pete's voice is firm, "Siri, call Logan."

The phone rings through the car's sound system, breaking the silence. Yeah, I'm pretty sure Bluetooth technology didn't exist back in the 1960's. According to re-runs, the best the 1960's had to offer for cellular technology was Maxwell Smart's shoe phone. I still want one of those.

After a couple of rings, we hear a resounding click. A male voice mumbles, "Mrphmph! Hello?" Whoever he is, he was obviously sleeping.

"Great. You're awake. Logan, it's Pete. Be in my quarters in forty-five minutes and bring your stuff." Wow. That was curt.

"No."

"It wasn't a request, Logan. Be there in forty-five and bring your equipment. I need your help with... something." Pete keeps his eyes on the road. He has a severe look on his face as he speaks. Pete clenches and relaxes his jaw repeatedly, tightening his grip on the wheel as he does it.

"Pete, I'm not your fucking house nurse. I'm not going to be at the ready 24/7 to stitch you up after each of your barroom brawls. Get your shit together, do like everyone else, and wait in line at the ER. Call me if you're dying, but don't ever wake me up again just to fix up your pretty face."

Pete's nostrils flare like he's losing his temper. "It's not for me, it's for someone else." Pete's eyes glance my way briefly when he says this.

I'm not sure I like where this is going. I don't want anyone to know about tonight. I don't want anyone seeing me. I just wanted him to drop me off at Erin's apartment and be done with it all. I needed an escape plan and he was available. I open my mouth to interrupt their conversation, to protest, but he raises his right hand from the polished wood steering wheel, motioning for me to keep quiet. All righty then, mouth closed it is.

The man on the other line lets out a rush of air. "What do you mean, not for you? Jesus, Pete! Please don't tell me you knocked someone up? Keep it covered or keep it in your pants for chrissake! If you think I'm going to help you run your own private abor..."

Before the man can finish his sentence, Pete cuts him off of the sound system by placing the phone to his ear.

Okay, that was awkward. I bite my lip and look down at my battered hands, trying to stay in my own little bubble. Pete does have a reputation of being a lady's man. If you believe everything you read, he always has a different woman on his arm. It's a typical case of the rotten apple not falling far from the dead tree.

According to gossip, out of the three brothers, Sean, the oldest, is the hard-ass workaholic. Jonathan, the youngest, is the charismatic, yet impulsive fuckup. As for Pete, the middle child, well, he got his Dad's promiscuity and his Mom's short temper.

Their Dad has a constant string of mistresses that he flaunts, in front of his wife, no less. I know. I've seen it in person on various occasions. Some of these women are barely my age. Pete is just following in his Dad's footsteps, I suppose. I wouldn't know what to do if my Dad acted that way. It probably sucked for him as a kid, always seeing his parents apart and his dad with a new woman. That doesn't excuse his behavior, but it does offer a little insight into Pete now. People become what they see, and he wasn't shown much of anything good. His mother is a psycho and his dad is a whore. I imagine his childhood was pretty awful.

"Logan, it's not what you think. I have someone with me and she needs help." Pete's voice is stern, and he looks at me with an odd expression I can't quite place.

Logan must be saying something Pete doesn't like, because the muscles in his jaw twitch and his fingers of his right hand tighten around the phone, while his left hand grips the steering wheel increasingly harder. That's when I notice the thin white lines on his hands. Scars, old and new, marring the skin of his knuckles, proof he's been in multiple fights.

"No, I didn't... we didn't." He says through clenched teeth. I can see his patience snapping away, strand by strand. He's a wild card. The other side of Pete, the fighter, is starting to show through. He looks like he wants to inflict bodily harm to whoever is on the other end of the line.

Eventually, he sighs and rubs his eyebrows with the fingers of one hand. His temper seems to simmer down a smidgen. "She's not like that. I—owe it to her. It's the right thing to do. Please."

His eyes look straight into mine as he speaks, and it's all I can do not to squirm in my seat.

He owes it to me? What was that about? Since when does a Ferro owe anything to anyone?

Maybe it was just a ploy, or maybe this is his way of apologizing for having been rude to me earlier when he invited me for a *ménage à trois* with the red head?

That's doubtful. It's something else. Pete's dark gaze darts back to the road.

"Thanks. I owe you one. Bring whatever

you would need for burns and don't mention this to anyone." Done with his call, Pete reaches over and puts the phone in the cradle in front of me. His arm brushes against mine and I'm suddenly very aware of his proximity, the heat radiating off of his body in the close quarters. I mean, the man is attractive, after all. There's a reason why women are always flocking to him.

I can totally see the appeal. Tall, strong, reckless, handsome, the bluest eyes ever, kissable lips...

He's impossibly hot. No wonder why Erin calls him a sexy beast. Beautiful and strong. Rare combo. Too bad there are no brains in there.

"Pete, you shouldn't take me home. In fact, you should drop me at my friend's house."

He laughs. "The grinder girl?" I don't get it. He smirks. "Your friend had fun shaking her ass between two guys all night. She probably doesn't even know there was a fire."

"You saw who I was standing with?"

"I saw you. She was noticeable."

That's not the word used to describe

Erin. I stare a hole in the side of his face waiting for more, but he doesn't offer.

"Whatever. Drop me at her place. I can't go home with you. People will talk and my parents will have you castrated. I don't want to fend off the swarm of women hoping to have your babies, so just drive me to Erin's."

Pete laughs that deep chuckle of his. He glances at me quickly, amused. "I didn't think you'd be into that."

"Into what?"

"Your friend left with them. Odds are she's getting nasty right now. If you walk in on that you'll imply you're open."

"Open?"

"Yeah, like you're open for business. Wrong message, Princess. Besides, everyone is asleep or passed out. Reporters can't get on the mansion grounds, and Logan can discreetly help you with that cough and the other stuff. If you want to keep this between us, fine. Believe me, I can't let people know I was seen with you. It'd ruin my image. You're a fucking nun." The corner of his mouth pulls up and he steals a glance my way.

I huff and try not to look at him.

Arrogant asshole. He's right, but that doesn't mean I have to like it. "Fine, but let me call Erin. She's dumb enough to run into the rubble looking for me."

"Or call your parents." Pete smiles and shakes his head. "Stop pretending you have no motives."

"I don't have motives, you just don't need to know my business. And I could have been in a four-way." Pete smiles, but doesn't respond. I prattle on, irritated at his assumption of my purity. I'm not a nun. I could be slutty. "For all you know, I'm a nympho and I was trolling for fresh meat."

Pete busts a gut laughing, which immediately turns into a coughing fit. My hand flies to slap his arm, but by the time it makes contact, he's dealing with the aftermath of the smoke. I rest my palm on his arm for a second.

"Sorry. Are you okay?"

His gaze drops to my hand and then trails up my arm and to my face. His eyes dart between the road and my touch. I pull away because I can't read the look he's giving me. Tucking my hair behind my ear, I glance at his phone.

"Can I call my friend?"

Pete keeps his eyes on the road as he considers my request. Without a word, he reaches over and I feel him brush up against me once more. That feeling is still there, that awareness of having him so close, the sense of his warmth. My fingers twitch, wanting to touch him again, just a little bit.

"Yes, you're safe. I'll make sure of it. What's your friend's number?"

I blink, not realizing that he is no longer reaching in front of me, but sitting straight behind the steering wheel once more, pushing buttons on his screen, smirking. Does he know what I was just thinking? I clear my throat and feel my face burning up. What the heck is wrong with me tonight? I shake the feeling off and give him Erin's number. The ringing comes through the sound system once more.

"Hello?"

"Hey, Erin, it's me." I try to talk as loud as I can so that she can hear me, but my voice is still fairly weak.

"Holy freaking hell! Gina! Are you okay? Where are you? I was looking all over for you! I went outside to have a smoke and then all hell broke loose. I couldn't find you outside, so I came back to my place, but you weren't here either and you weren't answering your cell and I thought you were dead and I practically crapped my pants I was so worried! Don't do that to me again, bitch!" Her voice is frantic, screeching, words coming out rapidly without a breath in between them.

"Erin, Erin! Stop! I'm ok. I made it out of the building safely." And then it hits me. I made it out of the building safely. But how? I was locked up, in a remote room, and I'm fairly certain I was unconscious. When I came to, I was outside in Pete's arms. Did he get me out? If so, why and how? How did he know to look in that tiny hidden space? He saved my life.

"Where are you, Gina? I'm coming to get you."

"No. Don't. I'm fine. Listen. Whatever you do, don't mention my name to anybody and stick to the original plan. I'll make sure I get back to your place... soon, and then we'll figure out what to do with my father. Just don't worry about me okay?"

"If you say so. Are you sure you're

okay?"

"Yes, Erin. I'll be just fine."

Erin lets out a snort, "This has been quite the night, huh?" Her voice has a bit of a smirk to it. Leave it to her to find the humor in something so horrific.

"Yes, it has." My voice is more somber than hers, and we both go silent for a while. Eventually, I hear her stretching and yawning on the other end.

"Well, I don't know about you, but I'm beat and in need of a distraction. I think I may take a little trip downstairs to Ricky's before catching some zzz's. You know, take the edge off a bit? Hey! I think I may pretend he's Pete and think about how Ferro was driving it home tonight. Man that was hot as Hades! He can ram into me in a dark corner like that any day. You gonna picture that next time you're stuck starfishing with Dr. Missionary?"

Oh.

My.

GOD!

If my eyes could pop out of my skull they would. With those few words, Erin took mortification and brought it up to levels of epic proportion. I dive for the phone, wanting desperately to hang up on her and end this nightmare of a phone call, but my seat belt jams and throws me back against the seat. The impact makes me start another fit of coughing, and Pete grabs the phone before I can. I reach out and try to swat at him repeatedly, desperately trying to grab that phone. He even has the audacity to chuckle. I'm dying of embarrassment, and the man is frigging laughing!

"Hey. It's Erin, right? Hi, Erin. Pete Ferro, here. Just to let you know, I'll be taking *very* good care of your friend Gina. She's in extremely good hands. You don't have to worry about a thing." The way he says it, it's laced with sexual innuendos of the sexy sexual type. "Oh, and by the way, I'm glad you found me so inspiring, but there is NO substitute for the real thing. Just sayin'."

Pete smiles a wicked, crooked smile and hangs up, but not before I can hear Erin let out a high pitched "eeep".

NO SUBSTITUTIONS OR EXCHANGES

3:21 am

Pete leads us silently through the endless maze of hallways inside the Ferro mansion. The interior is stunning. I had seen the grounds before during social events, but had yet to set foot inside. I catch my reflection in an intricate gilded mirror somewhere down one of the hallways. I'm a mess. I look like a hobo. My white sleeveless blouse is tattered and stained, my hair looks like road kill and my mascara has run down my cheeks, leaving dark black streaks along my face. Pete, on the other hand, looks wonderfully rumpled and filthy. Life is so unfair. His hair is a beautiful floppy brown mess, and his soot-stained face makes him look like he's Mr. June in a sexy firefighters calendar.

He eventually stops in front of a door and turns to face me. I try to tame the wild animal that has taken refuge in my hair, and Pete just grins. I want to smack him. Jerk.

When he opens the door and leads me in, I stop in my tracks. It's a massive bathroom equipped with a gigantic shower of polished white stone, and an exquisite bath. After the night I've had, my body is aching to crawl into it and soak for hours. As with everything in this place, the tub is huge. It could easily sit four people very comfortably. I try not to think about how many people he's actually been able to entertain in it. In fact, I'm trying so very hard not to think about how I'm in an opulent bathroom with a beautiful man who is not my boyfriend and who is probably considering entertaining me in here as well. After the phone call fiasco with Erin, who knows what's going on in this guy's head? What the hell am I doing here?

Pete takes out not one, but two folded bundles from the cabinet and hands them to me.

My stomach is twisting in knots and I'm exhausted. Our fingers touch very briefly, and the caress is to die for. Instantly I blurt out, "I HAVE A BOYFRIEND!" I cringe as soon as the words come out. Oh yeah, I'm so smooth.

Pete lets out a laugh and shakes his head before saying teasingly, "Yes, and your friend Erin speaks very highly of him. Actually, I was thinking that maybe you would like to freshen up a bit before Logan gets here." After I shoot him a panicked look that is the equivalent of screaming *I'm not into gang bangs*, he laughs and explains, "He's a doctor and my cousin, I trust him. The least I can do is make sure you get some help before I send you on home, and he's promised not to say anything to anyone."

Okay, so now I feel like a moron. I automatically jump to the conclusion that he wants to jump me when all he's trying to do is help me. I need a nap and a new brain.

Pete points to the shower adding, "You

should find everything you need in there. Will you be okay on your own?" His voice is no longer teasing, so I know he's not offering to give me a sponge bath. He adopts a sense of reverence, like I'm untouchable, too respectable to be looked at. I don't like it.

Maybe I'm reading him wrong. I can't tell.

"I should be fine. I'm feeling better than I was earlier, but thank you for your concern." My voice catches when I start to talk, but I quickly recover.

Pete offers a friendly nod. "All right. I'll be back soon, then." He turns away towards the door, but hesitates before leaving. After scanning my body up and down, then moistening his bottom lip with the tip of his tongue, he flashes a salacious grin and gives me a wink. "Are you sure you don't need any help? You're not the only one who needs a little... cleaning up and I'm very thorough. Maybe we can help each other feel... refreshed." With that, he removes his shirt slowly, as if he was a male stripper, slowly teasing it up over his head.

"Omigod! Get out!" Before he has time

to take a step closer, he gets hit in the face with one of the towels he handed me.

Taking the hint, Pete laughs and leaves the room, closing the door behind him. I'm left alone, holding the other white fluffy towel, with thoughts of him... naked, wet and covered in suds. A smile tugs at my lips. What an idiot. He's teasing me and seems to like it. I'm sure he knows he'll get a rise out of me.

My mind strays back to Anthony. There's no playful banter between us, nothing like this. It's safe to assume Pete doesn't like me that way, but he likes taunting me. I'm nun material, not something he wants to nail to the wall.

He's just being nice. There's nothing weird about this, but it feels weird. I shove the thoughts aside, strip and kick my clothes toward the door. The thought of putting them back on and smelling like a smoked pig again isn't appealing. As the steamy water hits my face, I grab a bottle of body wash. After squeezing it into my palm, the scent hits me. Holy shit, it's Pete Ferro in a bottle. I glance at it, wondering what it is, but it's not a name brand and the label is in

Italian. Maybe he patented it, "Ferro Wash, for all your dirty parts." I laugh at my fake slogan and shut off the shower.

Feeling more like a human being, I step out of the shower and gently towel off, making sure not to aggravate any wounds. After a very unladylike session of coughing up crap from my lungs, I reach for my clothes, but they are gone. In their place is a white fluffy robe, the Ferro family crest embroidered on the left breast.

The fact that someone came into the bathroom while I was in the shower doesn't go unnoticed. I pull on the robe, wrapping myself in its soft white fluffiness, and tie the belt tightly around my waist. Thanks to the person who took off with my clothes, I'm going commando and feeling more than a bit self-conscious.

After untangling my long brown hair with my fingers, I step into the corridor, barefoot. Pete is waiting for me, leaning against a wall, reading a book with a pen clamped between his teeth. He's ditched his clothes from earlier, and is now wearing a pair of dark blue lounge pants and a white V-neck shirt that clings to his muscular chest. His hair is wet and slicked back. Of course, he looks freshly showered and ready for bed. Pete's scent fills the air, and my stomach dips with the realization that we smell alike. It implies something intimate happened, even though it's not like that.

When Pete sees me approach, he smiles and closes his book, placing the pen inside to mark his page and tucking it under his arm. To my surprise, he extends a hand, "Hi, I'm Pete Ferro. Pleased to meet you. And you are?" His eyes have a bit of a gleam and the corner of his mouth lifts on one side, offering a friendly smile.

"Where are my clothes?" Yeah, I'm not going to win the prize for Miss Congeniality this year. Despite his attempt at friendly chitchat, I'm feeling very vulnerable, not to mention drafty in the nether regions.

I want my clothes.

Maybe Pete is one of those creepers who keeps trophies from each conquest. Maybe he has drawers full of women's underwear and mine are the new addition? They'd be smokin' hot. Bad pun. I'm too tired. My mind turns to pun pudding after two in the morning.

Pete's smile turns mischievous, and he takes another step forward. That scent fills the air between us. A coy look crosses his face, like he knows what I'm thinking, and how nervous he makes me.

"I've sent them to be laundered. They'll be brought back to you when they are ready. However," he walks slowly around me, and I can feel his eyes appraising me up and down, "I like this look on you much better. Less hassle."

He flicks a finger at the neckline of my robe, and I clutch it tightly to keep it shut. Gone is the man who was taking care of me before, and I am now confronted with the playboy the tabloids love to write about. This is the man who constantly tries to bed women, and he's not looking at me like I'm his little sister anymore. I swallow hard, feeling the sting in my throat, and step back.

Pete steps toward me, closing the space, and extends his hand once more, "Now, seeing that we got off on an unusual start, let me do this again. Pete Ferro, and you are?"

I tentatively place my hand in his, and he gives it a bit of a gentle squeeze. Despite his smugness, he's being careful not to hurt me. "Gina Granz."

He hums to himself once and releases my hand. We continue our trek through the mansion, me in a robe, Pete in his pajamas. He leads us into what appears to be a study, and stands in the doorway, letting me go in first.

"Have a seat and make yourself comfortable. I'll be right back." He motions towards a dark leather couch in the center of the room.

Make myself comfortable? I'm not naïve, I've seen movies. When a man asks a woman to make herself comfortable, it usually involves lingerie and a sexy pose that feels ridiculous.

"I meant, have a seat and relax. Damn, are you always this uptight?"

My jaw drops. "Are you always so rude?"

"No, it's only after saving women who drown themselves in my body wash so they can secretly take me home with them." The corners of his mouth twitch like he wants to smile. "Do we have a little crush, Miss Granz?"

"You wish. I'd rather smell like smoke

than you. I didn't realize what it was until I already dumped it out."

His face drops. "You poured my soap down the drain?"

I can't help it, I grin. What's with him and this magical cologne? "Maybe," I lie. "Was it infused with your body oil or something?"

"You can't dump it down the drain! That stuff was like $800 for a little bottle!" He glances back at the bathroom with a forlorn expression on his lips. Is he pouting? I let him suffer for a second longer, then let him off the hook.

"I'm not crazy, Pete. I didn't trash your stash of metrosexual products."

"I'm not a metro." I lift my eyebrows and fold my arms over my chest, making his eyes lower for a second, before meeting my gaze.

"Then what's with the soap and the custom stuff?"

He grins a little bit, like he's totally busted, and turns his back on me. "A guy just likes certain things, that's all. I had that scent made for me in this little shop in Venice."

"To woo a woman through her nose."

He grins. "Maybe." Something's changed in those moments. The lightness of the moment took away everything else and it felt like he was a real person, not the fist-flinging Ferro depicted on the television. "Like I said, have a seat, and don't worry, Gina, I won't bite." He says it with a friendly and reassuring tone, easing my nerves somewhat, but adds, "Not unless you ask me to."

He waggles his eyebrows as he disappears through the same door we came in.

The smell of new leather and old books fills the air. Wooden shelves line the walls, and there's a massive mahogany desk at the far end of the room. I pad over to the couch and take a seat, making sure the robe is tightly tucked around my legs. Tapping the tips of my sore fingers nervously on my knees, I look around and spot a pile of books on the side table next to me. Curiosity gets the better of me. I pick up the pile and stare at the authors, slightly amazed.

They're all famous poets.

The pages all have scribbled bits of paper sticking out of them, as if the reader was taking massive amounts of notes while reading. This can't be his. Pete likes poetry?

Just as he comes back into the room, I put the books down and readjust my robe, making sure no bits are showing. He is followed by a tall man, who must be his cousin Logan. The family resemblance is noticeable. He's carrying a large duffle bag, which he sets down beside me. Holding out a hand, he introduces himself as Dr. Ferro.

Logan carries himself with all the professionalism you would expect from a doctor. He is gentle, yet efficient, tending to the burns and splinters on my hands, then the scrapes on my legs, never pushing for more information than I am willing to give. He takes the time to listen to my breathing and check my vital signs. When he places a small clamp with a red light on the tip of my finger he explains that it's to check the oxygen levels in my blood. I stifle a giggle. I'd love to wave it in his face and say "E.T. phone home!" but I resist the urge. I don't want him admitting me to the hospital for brain damage or oxygen deprivation.

Pete sits at his desk, pretending to read, but I can tell he's watching us intently, rubbing his bottom lip with his index finger. I feel his eyes on me and can't help but wonder what's going on in his head. This man is a mystery. He's been genuinely gentle and caring. The look of concern is unmistakable in his eyes, yet he's also being a douche, constantly throwing seductive comments at me. It's done lightly— teasingly, like he knows he doesn't have a snowball's chance in Hell of getting between my legs.

Before he leaves, Logan tells me how to take care of my wounds and what symptoms to look for in case smoke inhalation causes any trouble. He even goes so far as to suggest that Pete keep an eye on me for the next couple of hours, to make sure my condition doesn't deteriorate. With a slap on the back and a handshake, Pete thanks his cousin and shows him out the door. We are alone once more.

Wordlessly, Pete takes a seat at his desk and resumes his reading, as if I'm not here. This man is bipolar or tripolar or how many other poles a personality can have. Wanting to break the uncomfortable silence, I walk over to his desk and lean against it. He raises his eyes towards me, above the pages of the book, but still doesn't say anything.

I'm still very much on edge from everything that's happened tonight. I don't have patience for his moody silent treatment. "So, what now?"

Pete closes his book, puts it down on his desk and, leaning back in his chair, puts both hands behind his head. "Now, we wait for your clothes to be ready and I drive you wherever you want to go. Unless you'd rather leave in that?"

Subtlety is not his thing, and he overtly checks out my attire. I bring my hands to the front of the robe, frowning, as I clutch the bottom and top firmly closed. "That's what I figured. Until your clothes are ready, feel free to rest on the couch or grab a book." He sits up straight in his chair, arms folded across his chest, giving me a look that makes me nervous. "Unless you had anything *else* in mind to help pass the time?"

Cocking my head to the side, I smirk and answer, "As tempting as that sounds, I do have standards, oh and that thing, what's it called again?" I tap my finger on my bottom lip, as if I'm trying to remember something. "Oh yeah, morals. I have a boyfriend, remember? I'm not having sex with you." I shrug a shoulder at him, trying to look as smug as I can.

He gets up from his chair and saunters over to my side of the desk, putting me more on edge. Maybe taunting him wasn't such a good idea after all. With the desk acting as a physical barrier between us, it was so much easier to put up a strong front and he knows this. Well, if he thinks he can break me with his sexy self-assured walk, his perfectly toned muscles and his beautifully tempting smile, he has another thing coming.

Pete rubs the stubble on his jaw with the back of one hand. "Yes, well, according to your friend on the phone, it seems that your boyfriend may be lacking in some areas." His lips curve into a presumptuous expression that I want to smack off of his face. Okay, so first thing tomorrow morning, I'm killing Erin for that starfishing comment she made on the phone!

"Maybe I can assist you with that

problem? It's amazing what a good fucking can do to a person. But you probably wouldn't know that, would you?" He asks, taking a step closer. Pete knows he's sexy, and his words hit my buttons dead center. It's strange how his words both offend and excite me. No one has ever talked to me like that before.

I start to laugh, because I'm a nervous wreck and he's obviously joking, trying to get me to react, but when I see that the smirk on his face is gone, I stop and my face drops. "Wait, you're serious. You're actually asking me to cheat on him? With you?"

"Why not?" Peter shrugs as if it doesn't matter.

"Uh, because... boyfriend! That's why not!" He shakes his head like he just doesn't get it. "Hello? Pete Ferro meet reality. Reality, meet Pete Ferro. People don't do that when they're in a relationship with somebody else. At least not normal people. You should only have that kind of intimacy with the person you love. Otherwise, what's the point? Isn't sex supposed to be the ultimate expression of someone's love for another person?"

Pete takes a couple more steps towards me and leans back against the desk next to me. "Ah... love. I see where you may be confused. I wasn't offering to make love to you. I offered to fuck you, thoroughly and hard. Sex isn't love. Don't ever make the mistake of confusing the two. Sex is a powerful, physical thing. Once you start mixing in stupid notions of love, it kills the passion."

Heart racing, my jaw drops. I snap out of it. "Jaded much?"

"No, realistic much.

"Tell me no more of minds embracing minds,
And hearts exchang'd for hearts;
That spirits meet, as winds do winds,
And mix their subt'lest parts;
That two unbodied essences may kiss,
And then like Angels, twist and feel one Bliss.

I was that silly thing that once was wrought
To practice this thin love;

Come, I will undeceive thee, they that tread
Those vain aerial ways

Are like young heirs and alchemists misled
To waste their wealth and days,
For searching thus to be forever rich,
They only find a med'cine for the itch."

The poem is raw and crude and the way Pete recites it is powerful.

"You left out a few parts, Pete."

"Alas, they prove my point, Gina Granz. Love is an illusion for feeble minds who give way to the whims of the wind." Smirking, he takes the book from me and puts it on his desk. I can feel the passion in his eyes and in his voice as he speaks.

"You don't believe that, do you?" I'm curious now. How can anyone get through life with such a jaded perception of reality? "Love is real. It binds all things, holding us together and giving us life."

"No, a sperm and an egg gave you life. Love had nothing to do with it." Pete works his jaw, like he's trying to decide whether or not he should say something.

"Go on, then. Enlighten me." I tip my head to the side, surprised by the sharp mind working in that pretty head.

As he steps closer, those impossibly blue

eyes bore into me. "What it all comes down to is primal, physical need. We are hot-blooded creatures meant to feel passion, hunger, pain, hate, euphoria, fear and lust. Right now, you are using love as a way to justify what your body craves, to ease your conscience, instead of seeing it for what it really is."

I smile a little, amused at myself for feeling torn between shock that he's intelligent and shock at his view of things. "And what is it?"

Pete is in my face, lips close enough to kiss. His breath washes over me when he speaks, and my silly smile falls from my face and shatters. "It's plain, physical need. We all need to eat to survive, Gina. Do we settle on basic bread and water our whole lives, or do we indulge in other foods that taste more pleasant to the palate? Your views on sex and love are hypocritical and wasteful. In fact, your storybook notion of love is killing your passion until one day, all you'll feel for each other is numbness and resentment. And where will that leave you? It leaves you with a husband who satisfies his hunger for lust outside of your sacred love.

"Why would anyone want to put themselves through any of that? Case in point, what your friend said about your beloved boyfriend. I'm willing to bet you've never screamed his name out loud while he made you come over and over again. You probably feel like every moment has to be tender, and saying dirty things out loud, asking him to do unspeakable things to your body will sully your precious relationship.

"You are repressed. You're holding yourself back. I can see it in your eyes. The passion is there, but you feel you can't be that person with him. *That* is what love does to passion and lust. It obliterates everything."

I can't answer and don't want to give him the satisfaction of admitting that, to some extent, he's right. Anthony and I have never had a very passionate love life, but it's caring. The thought of asking him to do things to me is a bit daunting, but that doesn't mean that it'll never happen. I'm sure Anthony and I can get there, one day, if that's what we both want.

When I don't answer, Pete says, "That's what I thought." He pauses and turns to face me, all intensity gone, and his grin back full wattage. He claps his hands together loudly once, and then rubs them together in anticipation. "So! Now that we have all that confusion sorted out, let me ask you again. Wanna fuck?"

FUCKAHOLICS ANONYMOUS

3:45 am

I choke on my spit, but my throat is too dry and still very sore, sending me into a fit of excruciatingly painful coughs.

Who asks that?

I bend over at the waist, wrapping one arm around myself, trying to keep my ribs from cracking, my other arm over my face.

Wordlessly, Pete steps around me and leaves the room. When he returns, I'm still coughing madly, trying desperately to catch my breath, but I can't. If I don't stop coughing soon, I'll surely faint from lack of oxygen. Pete grabs me by the waist, lifting me up and sits me down on the top of the desk. After handing me a glass of water, he puts a comforting hand on my back and looks at me with a worried expression on his face, eyebrows pinched, lips pressed together into a thin line.

He stays next to me like that, rubbing my back and saying soothing things, until the coughing finally dies down. I take a sip of water and thank him. I'm sitting on his desk, legs dangling off the edge and he's standing close enough for me to feel the heat radiating off of his body. I'm still trying to catch my breath as he dips down to look at me.

"Hey, I didn't think I'd set you off like that. Do you want me to call Logan back?" His voice is once more full of concern.

"You didn't. It's not you." I snap at him, and he smiles faintly.

He lifts his palms toward me. "Sorry, I was teasing. I didn't mean for you to choke up a lung. Are you sure you're okay?"

Our eyes lock and my stomach fills with something light. It's as if the air around us is charged and tugging us together. The thought scares the crap out of me. I can't like him. He's an asshole. But he's not. That's the problem. There are two Pete Ferros, the charming man in front of me now and the crude fuckaholic.

Pressing my lips together, I look away, breaking the moment. "No, it's okay. I should be fine now. Thanks."

Pete offers a shy smile. His words from earlier keep nagging at me. What if I do have it all wrong? What if sex isn't an expression of love, but just a primal bodily need meant to be satisfied, like hunger? Dammit. Now he's got me questioning myself.

"Lust and love can coexist." My voice is firm, certain.

"When you have proof, feel free to show me." The topic is closed now, like one of his old books.

The atmosphere in the room has gotten so tense with anticipation, you'd need an axe to cut through it.

I squirm on the desk and clear my throat while pointing at the desktop. "Just a quick question. I'm a little worried about my health after sitting on this desk. When you've had guests of the female variety over, do you disinfect this desk when you're done, uh, entertaining them on it?" I scrunch my nose to accentuate my disgust and mock-shudder. "Because I don't see any Lysol around. Gotta know if I need a cootie shot."

Pete's mouth quirks up into a half grin, and he shakes his head. When he opens his mouth to say something, I cut him off. "No way. Wait! Let me guess!"

I put a finger up so that he doesn't interrupt me, and cross my legs while tossing my hair dramatically behind my shoulders.

Putting on a straight face, I'm going for alpha-male serious as I stare up at him from under my lashes. Pete looks amused as I try to do my best impersonation of a dark and brooding man, my voice husky and low, "This study is my sacred place, my sanctuary. I never bring women in this room, you are the first. All those other women? They are insignificant. They have only seen my bedroom. That is where I fuck them thoroughly and hard. You, are special." I can't make it to the end without laughing. I break character as I reach the part about the bedroom.

Smiling, Pete applauds my performance, so I take a small bow atop the desk, grinning.

"Impressive but wrong. If you must know, I never bring any women home at all. Laugh all you want, but you're the first."

"Oh man, so is there nothing sacred, then? Have I made you break your Golden Rule? How does it go? Is it something like, *Thou shalt not bring forth wenches and strumpets in thy sanctuary?* Well, lucky for you, I'm neither a wench nor a strumpet. But still," I place my hand in front of his face as if I'm holding a microphone and I'm a reporter interviewing him "Mr. Ferro, inquiring minds want to know, are there any rules that you haven't broken yet, be it moral, social, personal or legal?"

He chuckles and pushes my fake microphone hand away. Flicking back his head he sends wet strands of brown hair flying back. "Actually, if you must know, there is one last personal rule. And I'll never break that one." He rocks back and forth on his heels, with an air of arrogance that is just begging to be egged on.

"Really? And what would that rule be, Mr. Ferro, and does it involve another man and your ass?" I put my microphone hand back in front of his face.

Pete makes a *tsk, tsk* sound and waves a finger. "That's my little secret. What about you, Miss Granz? What's your golden rule?"

He wraps his fingers around my hand and brings it towards my face as if he's interviewing me instead. He's looking at me as if I'm dessert. I try to act as if I'm unaffected, but the truth is, when he looks at me that way, he makes me feel desirable, which is something I'm not used to.

Loved? Yes.

Appreciated? Most definitely.

Desired? Never.

I need to be more careful around him. I need to put some space between us. I don't trust myself anymore, not with this man who has beauty and brains. It's a deadly combination.

I try to get off of the desk, but he takes a step closer making it impossible for me to stand without pressing up against his body, which is something I am not going to do. He is so close I can feel his chest brush against my robe when he breathes.

When he looks down at me, strands of wet hair flop back down onto his forehead. Little drops of water form on the ends and drip down onto my robe-covered knees. His smile fades and his gaze darkens, "It would bring me great pleasure to break some of your precious little rules."

My confident smile falters. "Well, good luck with that. I'm not a rule breaker. Clean slate. Miss Straight-and-Narrow, right here. The perfect daughter, girlfriend, student, employee, you name it."

I make it sound as if I like it, as if I'm proud, and tick them off on my fingers one-by-one. I sound confident, but deep down, mountains of regret and lost opportunities press on top of me, pushing me deeper into the ground. Most of the time I feel like a puppet and everyone is pulling on a different string—everyone except for me. It's like I don't have a say in who I should be or what I should do. I'm so tired of trying to be perfect for everyone.

I look down, my hair falling in curtains around my face. I'm flicking at the corner of one of my bandages with a finger.

Pete uses one hand to push back my hair and the other to gently lift my chin. "Ah, but you're not Little Miss Perfect. You did break the rules. You were at an illegal party tonight, when you could have chosen to be anywhere else. See? Rules are meant to be broken, Gina. Even the ones we hold onto the most. Learn to let go. Your life is too short to spend it holding back all the time."

Pete's gaze intensifies before he closes his eyes and quotes softly,

"When you are old and grey and full of sleep,
And nodding by the fire, take down this book,
And slowly read, and dream of the soft look
Your eyes had once, and of their shadows deep;

How many loved your moments of glad grace,
And loved your beauty with love false or true,
But one man loved the pilgrim soul in you,
And loved the sorrows of your changing face;

And bending down beside the glowing bars,
Murmur, a little sadly, how Love fled
And paced upon the mountains overhead
And hid his face amid a crowd of stars."

"That's beautiful. Who wrote that?" I exhale, taken aback. The way he recites this poem is both melodious and melancholy. It flows like a dance off of his tongue, where the other poem was forceful and fiercely intense.

"Yeats. It's a reminder not to waste your youth. Don't let yourself get hung up on what's right or wrong. Let yourself be desired, even if it isn't true love. Life is too short, Gina. Of all people, you should know this better than anyone now."

Being locked in that room, alone, waiting to die, was the single most terrifying experience of my life. Yet, despite the fear of dying, all I could think about is how I haven't done a single thing in my life worth remembering. I've spent my life attempting to live up to everybody else's expectations of me.

I want to feel something real for a change. For me. Is it wrong to want to cut those strings and purposefully do the wrong thing once in a while? I want to be free to do what I want, when I want, to be wild for a moment and not care about the consequences.

But what Pete is asking me to do, I just can't. I can't be unfaithful to Anthony. Just the fact that I'm having this internal debate in the first place is all sorts of wrong.

Or is it? In the grand scheme of things, when your time comes and life is over, does it matter if you've thrown your personal values away to succumb to temptation? What happens if I waste my life because I've clung to values too tightly? Will I regret saying no to Pete? Will there be a million *what if's* that dance through my mind at night?

My silence speaks loudly. I don't have a quirky comeback or a sassy remark. I don't say anything. I want to look down, but Pete keeps my chin up with his finger and he's searching my eyes for any kind of sign.

Pete's voice is as deadly as a siren's song. He lulls me, making things twist away from what I thought they should be. His words swirl around my mind as his palms warm my face. A breath away, he asks, "Can you tell me, in all certainty, that you don't have the least little bit of desire? That there's nothing between us?" Pete is silent for a while, but when I don't answer, he raises an eyebrow, slightly cocking his head to the side, waiting. He runs a gentle finger along my cheek.

The response is immediate and all consuming. Butterflies swirl within me, begging to be freed. I can't think. I don't know what to do. He makes sense, but this isn't me. Is it? I can't tell anymore.

All I have to do is say the word and this very sexual man could be mine for the night. It's tempting, knowing he's a sure thing. I could do this and never see him again. No one would ever know. I could feel raw, unadulterated passion. Oh, the things he could teach me, the things he could do to my body.

But can I detach my body from my heart and just have sex with a stranger? Can I be unfaithful and live with myself afterwards?

He's not a stranger anymore.

THE BROKEN RULE

4:12 am

The thought vibrates through my mind. In that moment, I realize something changed. Earlier in the evening he was a random person, some guy I noticed. Now he's not. Now he's a warm touch, and a pair of safe, strong arms. I want to know where his affection for poetry originated. I want to know him. It bothers me. I try to shake it off, because it's insane. No one knows this guy. Besides, good girls aren't his type.

"I can't." It's an ambiguous answer. I won't lie and I can't say that I haven't had any desire to give in to him. The desire is there, but I can't do this. Some lines shouldn't be crossed and this line is one of them.

But Pete thinks my answer is consent. He closes the distance between us, his body inching toward mine. He places his hands on both my knees and spreads them apart, just enough to let him get closer in between my thighs.

From that one touch, a shiver swallows me whole. I expected him to be forceful, but he's anything but that. The caress steals my breath, and after everything we've been through tonight, I feel like I know him, like walking away will be a loss. I can't explain it, because it makes no sense. We're too different, but he's here with that endearing grin and that damned dimple.

His palm is warm, and rests on the top of my thigh. I stiffen, trying to resist him. I try to push against his hands, but I'm too shaky. As I move, the robe shifts, and I still. Worry swirls in my stomach, pooling with lust that's burning hotter than the warehouse. The look in his eyes isn't the same as when he devoured the redhead. It makes me want to say yes. Pete makes me reconsider everything.

Heat pools in my forbidden areas against my will. It doesn't matter how many times I mentally say no, because my body ignores me. Pete leans in closer and slides his hands over the robe, up my thighs and toward my hips. His fingers hug the curves of my ass over the fabric, truly feeling me like he wants to memorize that curve down to the last detail.

My breath hitches. My plan to pull away doesn't work—I can't do it. The desk is on one side and Pete is on the other. Words escape me and I wish things were different, but I can't do this. I have to say something to stop him. My head and my heart are screaming at me, telling me to push him away, but my body is clearly into him.

My eyes scan up and down his body slowly, wondering what he looks like underneath those clothes. I try to imagine every curve and dip of his toned muscles. I start chewing my lower lip and he must see the inner struggle going on inside my head, because he slows. He won't push me. His hands linger, waiting while his lips part.

That beautiful blue gaze fixates on my robe. He's undressing me with those perfect eyes. He's too close, and the heat coming off of him calls to me. Pete mixes with that body wash and it's hard not to lean in and inhale him.

I place both hands on his chest to push away. It doesn't matter how much I want to trail my fingers under his shirt and across his chest, to feel how smooth and hard he really is—I can't run my thumbs over his nipples and feel them harden from my touch. I won't.

I've never had these thoughts about anyone before. It catches me off-guard and instead of pushing him away, I linger. His eyes consume me and I want him so badly I think I may give in. He's breaking me, coaxing me to be someone I'm not and it scares me.

"I can't." My voice is a breath and I push against his chest, trying to shove him away from me, but it hurts. My wounds are bandaged, but they aren't healed.

When he speaks again, his voice sounds self-assured and arrogant, "I saw how you were looking at me earlier, when I was with that other woman. You want me, but you're too scared to admit it. Let go of your ridiculous principles; they're holding you back. It's only sex."

I laugh, but there's no mirth in it. Pete catches my lip between his fingers and the smile fades from my face. I tug away, freeing my mouth. "This is a game to you, and maybe at some other time I'd be willing to play, but don't ask me to betray myself. You ran into a burning building for me. Don't push me like this; we both know I'll break. Peter, please."

Using his full name does something to him and his cocky expression washes away. I see the passionate poet, the man who thinks love is a hoax. "What if it's not breaking? What if it's fate and this is our chance, Gina? What if you're here because that's what was supposed to happen? If you walk away, you'll never know. How can you live like that?"

I shake my head fervently, still pushing against his chest and he stares down at me intently, brushing a stray strand of hair off of my cheek. My eyes flutter closed for an instant, in hope that blocking him from my sight will help extinguish this unwanted fire building up inside of me, but it only heightens my other senses, making his touch more decadent. I need to move, but he's got me trapped on his desk with one hand on my backside and his whole body blocking me from the front.

I gasp and try to talk, but my rationality is failing. "I'm pretty sure that line only works on high school girls."

Pete laughs. "That's not what I meant. Two people meet by chance, the way we did —do you really think this is nothing?"

I tense and look at his perfect mouth, thinking. "It's something."

"Then say it, tell me to stop and I will." As he speaks, he presses his fingertip to my cheek and slides it along my jaw, down my throat, over my collar bone until he's drifting along the neckline of my robe where it plunges down toward my chest.

My breasts scream for his attention, begging for his hand to dip under the fabric, but he doesn't. He keeps on trailing his fingers down lower until they reach the knot at the belt and I stop breathing altogether.

Time is suspended. My eyes close for a

moment, as I savor the sensation of his touch and the way his warm breath washes across my face. He smells so good, like sex and warmth.

"We shouldn't…" It's barely a whisper, but my plea is there.

Why won't he listen? He's so sure that this is what I want. Is he really so used to having women throw themselves at him, that he can't fathom someone would actually turn him down?

I open my eyes and stare at his parted lips, imagining him leaning in, imagining him kissing me, and the thoughts frightens me. I've already done so much tonight, this is wrong. I don't know what to do. My body is frozen in place, but my insides are burning. If I don't act now, he'll undo that knot, exposing my body to him. I don't think I'll have the resolve to push him away if things go that far. He'll be taking me, right here on this desk.

I'm assaulted by images of me screaming his name, my fingers tangled in his hair as he pushes into me, being taken in ways I've never been taken before, his mouth and his hands all over me. He is pure, sinful temptation. I doubt anyone has told him no before. There's an ache in my chest and I realize that it's from my heart pounding.

"Pete—"

I wiggle my hips on the desk, trying to get away from his grasp, pushing against his chest, but he takes my hands in his and brings them behind my back, holding both my wrists with one of his strong hands. He's looking straight into my eyes and, God, he's gorgeous! His blue eyes pop out in contrast with that perfectly sexy dark stubble along his jaw and I have the sudden urge to slap him for being so desirable, but I can't. He's holding me tightly and I can't break free.

"Gina—" Pulling me toward him on the desk, I'm pressed up against his body in a way that I can clearly feel how much he wants me. Shockingly, I can also tell that he is not the only one aroused. Feeling him so hard and ready, that exquisite pressure right on my already sensitive areas is enough to make me whimper.

At the sound, he closes his eyes for a moment and smiles. Part of me wants to move, to press into him more, to feel him. I don't, because a bigger part of me is angry my body is betraying me. I don't want to be this person.

"I'm not a slut. I don't do things like this. Pete…"

"You're not, I know. Believe me, I know. I'd never have a chance with a woman like you, not ever, but tonight went wrong and here we are. The question is, can you really tell me that you don't want this? I'll back away, right now." He scans me, waiting, but I don't respond.

All the things he said are flooding through my mind in a tornado, ripping away all my preconceived notions. Everything around us is quiet. The only sounds are our rapid breaths.

With silence as his only answer, Pete begins to step back and drops his hands. "Wait." My voice is small, almost not there.

Pete catches my eyes and sees my answer. He broke me. He actually got me to say it, to beg him to come back.

His eyes darken as his head dips toward my neck. His strong arms wrap around me, pulling me tightly into his chest. My thighs part and he's back where he was a moment ago. My head tips sideways, welcoming his lips and I moan softly without meaning to.

"That's it. Let go, Gina. Let your body do what it wants to. Give in."

His breath is so hot on my skin. His soft lips touch my neck, and I feel like I'm going to explode. That sexy mouth leaves a trail of flaming kisses along my neck, making me lean into his embrace. Another little whimper escapes my lips. I can feel the soft moistness of his tongue as it connects with the skin on my neck and the sharp bite of his teeth as he nibbles his way down.

One of Pete's hands is still holding mine firmly behind my back, while the other slides down my throat and grabs hold of my fluffy collar. His fingers dip inside, barely brushing my breast. The response is instant, I rock my hips into his once.

This time, my whimper is more like a soft moan as pressure slowly builds. I fight every natural instinct I have, holding myself back from rocking into him again and again. But it's hard, because I've never felt this way before. It's overpowering and all-consuming. I want it to stop, but only because I'm not supposed to like it so much.

Memories flash through my mind: the girl at the party, the way Pete held her against the wall, the way I imagined myself in her place while he kissed her neck and held her hands above her head, while he made love... no, fucked her, up against the wall.

This is not love. For Pete, this is fucking and it has nothing to do with sentimentality. If I don't stop this now, there won't be any going back. I'm about to say something, anything. But I can't. He caught me in his trap and I can't pull away, not anymore.

If I'd met the poet he's hiding inside that beautiful head, I would have fallen for him a long time ago. He's worth breaking up with Anthony. He's worth the risk, the heartache, everything—just to know him a little bit better, to be held in those arms for one night. I can't say no and realize I don't want to stop, but I have to.

I open my mouth, ready to tell him that, and take a deep breath, but Pete suddenly stops. He sucks in a shaky breath and backs away, letting my hands fall free.

His wild blue eyes are so torn, but I can't

imagine why. Breathing heavily, he takes a couple steps back and runs a hand across his face and through his hair, while studying me from the corner of his eyes. There is no mistaking the shape of his impressive length straining upwards under his light cotton pants.

When I look up to his face the spell is broken. He's flushed, but the look he gives me is a mixture of remorse and anger, like he regrets the past few moments.

"I can't do this," Pete breathes out through clenched teeth.

He looks at me like he's disgusted with me, like I'm the worst kind of tease. But I'm not. I never led him on, never once told him I wanted him. I pushed him back, told him to stop, tried to get away.

"It's all right." The words make me shiver inside. I've never, ever, put myself out there like that. But he seems so conflicted and I had to tell him that he read me right, that I do want him.

Pete shakes his head and has a spooked look in his eyes. Shaking his head, he backs away.

"Just—no, it's not. Okay? Just no."

"I don't understand. You just—"

He looks at me with an unreadable expression. There's only an inch between us, but it feels like miles. His brows are pinched together and he works his jaw while staring holes into my face. What did I do?

"I just can't do this because…" His voice trails off and he watches me for a second with a blank expression. Then his face scrunches up, he spins around and he punches the air, walking away from me as fast as he can. "It's you."

Pete leaves the room, slamming the door behind him, making me jump. Through the walls I hear him yell a loud, "FUCK!" Immediately following comes the sound of shattering glass.

AUTHOR'S NOTE

I'd like to say thank you to all of the Ferro fans who made this new series about Peter's past possible. Special thanks to Mike, who is always supportive, and my super-swicked kids! Thank you to Emerald the Awesome, for tackling everything at the last possible second with a smile. You rock!

A huge thank you to Melanie A Bussière who was a contributing editor, and my expert in all things Ferro, especially when it comes to Peter. I can't tell you how many times I've asked her for help and she's always there, ready to help me make Ferroaholics everywhere drool.

Finally, thanks to my family and friends who have all been a blessing during this time. The last year has been insane and I couldn't have made it through without you. Thank you!

~Holly

COMING SOON:

LIFE BEFORE DAMAGED 2
THE FERRO FAMILY

*****

To ensure you don't miss H.M. Ward's next book, text AWESOMEBOOKS (one word) to 22828 and you will get an email reminder on release day.

*****

Want to talk to other fans?
Go to Facebook and join the discussion!

COVER REVEAL

H.M. WARD

NEW YORK TIMES BESTSELLING SERIES

life before
DAMAGED
volume 3
DAMAGED

The FERRO Family

MORE FERRO FAMILY BOOKS

NICK FERRO
~THE WEDDING CONTRACT~
*****

BRYAN FERRO
~THE PROPOSITION~
*****

SEAN FERRO
~THE ARRANGEMENT~
******

PETER FERRO GRANZ
~DAMAGED~
******

JONATHAN FERRO
~STRIPPED~
******

MORE ROMANCE BY H.M. WARD

SCANDALOUS

SCANDALOUS 2

SECRETS

THE SECRET LIFE OF TRYSTAN SCOTT

DEMON KISSED

CHRISTMAS KISSES

SECOND CHANCES

And more.

To see a full book list, please visit:
www.sexyawesomebooks.com/#!/BOOKS

CAN'T WAIT FOR H.M. WARD'S NEXT STEAMY BOOK?

⭐⭐⭐⭐⭐

Let her know by leaving stars and telling her
what you liked about
LIFE BEFORE DAMAGED
in a review!

COVER REVEAL:

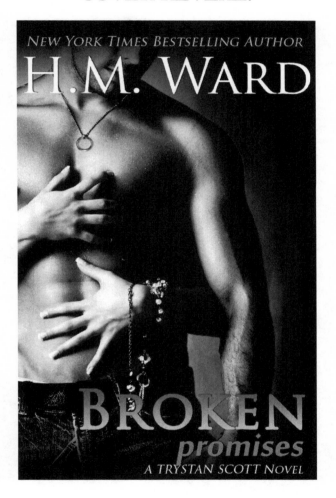

Made in the USA
Middletown, DE
29 November 2015